"You see, sweetheart, there's one big difference between your twisted admirer and me, and this is it."

Slowly Evan bent his head, oblivious to her sharply indrawn breath and the frightened widening of her blue eyes. His mouth touched hers very softly, as lightly as the drift of an autumn leaf falling to the ground. It touched, pressed, lingered for barely a moment, and then, just as Catherine felt herself respond helplessly, he broke the tiny erotic contact with brutal suddenness, lifting his dark head sharply and taking a step backward, away from her.

"You see, Cat, he would never be able to do this and walk away. But I can...."

KATE WALKER was born in Nottinghamshire, England, but as she grew up in Yorkshire she has always felt that her roots were there. She met her husband at university and she originally worked as a children's librarian, but after the birth of her son she returned to her old childhood love of writing. When she's not working, she divides her time between her family, their three cats, and her interests of embroidery, antiques, film and theater, and, of course, reading.

KATE WALKER

Flirting with Danger

Harlequin Books

TORONTO • NEW YORK • LONDON
AMSTERDAM • PARIS • SYDNEY • HAMBURG
STOCKHOLM • ATHENS • TOKYO • MILAN
MADRID • WARSAW • BUDAPEST • AUCKLAND

ISBN 0-373-11818-X

FLIRTING WITH DANGER

First North American Publication 1996.

Copyright © 1996 by Kate Walker.

CHAPTER ONE

THE sound of the doorbell rang loudly through the silent house, making Catherine tense instinctively. She froze in the middle of the room, her bright blue eyes wide with apprehension as her heart lurched into a heavy, painfully accelerated pounding so that she found it difficult to breathe naturally.

'Who is it?'

She struggled to form the words but her voice failed her, becoming just a thin thread of sound that wouldn't reach whoever was on the other side of the door.

'Who are you?' she tried again, with a little more success than before, but still not loudly enough to gain any response.

She would have to look through the peep-hole that her father had had installed, she told herself, ruthlessly squashing down the fear that held her paralysed. Only then would she know.

Know what? her mind flung at her, forcing her to face the brutal truth. How would she know if the caller at the door was the man she feared when she didn't even know his identity, had no idea what he looked like?

She had only hesitated a moment or two, struggling to regain enough control to be able to turn and move towards the hallway, but that short time was quite long enough for a key to be inserted in the lock, and she had just taken a couple of steps towards the hallway when the door swung open.

'Only me!'

Catherine's slim shoulders slumped under the impact of the sudden wave of relief that broke over her at the sound of her father's reassuring voice, her heart lifting in instinctive response, and the sense of dread vanishing like the mist before the sun at the sight of his smiling face. But almost immediately all her new-found ease fled as another man, big and dark-haired, stepped into the hall behind him, and all her tension and fear revived at the realisation that there was someone with her father— someone she neither knew nor recognised.

'Dad!'

Her voice was tight with the panic that the sight of an unknown face—particularly an unknown *male* face— could spark off in her so easily these days.

'Oh, I'm sorry darling.' Recognising her fear, Lloyd Davies' expression changed abruptly, apologetic concern showing in the blue eyes that were so like his daughter's. 'I should have thought—I asked Evan to come back with me, but I should have rung you first—'

'No—it's all right—' If her father could vouch for him, then surely she had nothing to fear.

But her voice lacked the conviction of truth, betraying her uncertainty in the way that it shook revealingly, and her state of mind was not made any easier by the disturbing realisation that the man called Evan was studying her with an interest that was positively laser-like in its intensity. His eyes—strange coloured eyes, neither blue nor green, but with the cold changeability of the sea on a winter's day—were narrowed assessingly as he watched her, and a frown creased the space between straight, dark brows.

'H-hello—'

Her weak attempt at a smile met with no response, and she was further unnerved by the way his considering gaze raked over her, from the top of her shining ash-blonde head to the toes on the bare feet that peeped out from beneath the ragged hems of the well-worn denim jeans that she wore with one of her father's old shirts, the faded pink cotton untucked at the waist and hanging loose around her narrow hips.

Her smile fading, she met that narrowed stare head-on, hiding behind a display of defiance the fact that she was quailing deep inside, her nerves twisting into tight, painful knots. She was used to public attention—in her job it was par for the course—but she certainly wasn't used to being subjected to such a deliberate scrutiny—particularly not when it was accompanied by such a frowningly disapproving expression.

'Evan who?' she asked, her voice more in control this time, though the determined effort she was making to smooth out the earlier unevenness made it sound cold and distant, earning her another of those swift, critical glances.

'Evan Lindsay,' he supplied, and the first sound of his voice was something of a shock. It was low and slightly husky, surprisingly soft when one considered that it came from such a big man.

And this Evan Lindsay was *big*. Her father stood a good six feet in his socks, but this man topped him by more than three inches—four, possibly, Catherine hazarded. The imposing height was matched by a similarly powerful frame, with broad shoulders and chest and long, strong arms.

The smartly tailored navy jacket and trousers, worn with a paler blue shirt and understated tie, might mirror the formal business suit Lloyd wore, but that formality emphasised rather than concealed the fact that the body underneath the fine cloth was definitely not that of a man who spent his day seated at a desk in some modern, high-tech office.

His face had the same sort of impact—hard-boned and strongly carved, with a distinct bump in the nose that told her it had once been well and truly broken and had had to be reset. Altogether, there was something about him that spoke of danger, of a powerful but vol-

atile force barely kept in check, like a half-tame tiger—
on the surface apparently quiet and controlled, but never,
ever totally trustworthy.

'Evan's been working on the alarm system at the
office,' her father put in in an obvious attempt to reassure her, ease the prickly atmosphere.

'Oh, so you're the new security man.'

She didn't even trouble to try to inject a note of polite
interest into her voice; as a matter of fact, her thoughts
weren't even on what she was saying. She saw now just
why her father had brought this man home with him;
exactly what had been in his mind at the time.

'I'm involved in the work, yes—'

'And I thought we could use some of Evan's expertise—'

'I don't think so,' Catherine cut in sharply. 'I don't
need any burglar alarms or security cameras—unless, of
course, you were proposing to act as a bodyguard?'

'I wasn't proposing anything.' The low voice held a
trace of something Catherine couldn't interpret—something that worried her. It might have been humour, but
if so it had a dark edge that tightened her nerves disturbingly. 'Lloyd simply asked me back here—'

'And I offered you a drink,' Catherine's father inter-
jected. 'But all I've done so far is keep you standing in
the hall. Why don't we go somewhere where we can sit
down and be more comfortable? The conservatory would
be pleasant—'

Catherine's involuntary movement drew his attention,
had him changing his mind.

'No, perhaps the lounge would be better. Cathy,
darling, why don't you take Evan through while I ask
Mrs Bentley to organise refreshments? Coffee, Evan?
Or would you prefer something alcoholic? And what
about something to eat?'

'Coffee would be fine—but, no, nothing to eat.'

Pushing back his shirt-cuff, Evan consulted a workmanlike watch on a slim leather strap.

'I'm meeting a friend in just over an hour. We're having dinner together.'

And he had no intention of being late, his attitude said only too clearly. As she led the way into the lounge Catherine couldn't help wondering a little about the friend he was obviously so concerned about. She—because it had to be a she—was obviously very important to him, and in spite of herself she found herself trying to imagine what sort of woman appealed to this man. Probably someone dark and fiery—exotically glamorous, very feminine, her looks the perfect foil to his forceful masculinity.

'I'm afraid you've had a wasted journey, Mr Lindsay.'

She spoke over her shoulder as she crossed to the large window in the far wall, pulling the blue velvet curtains more tightly shut with a swift, jerky action.

'We have a perfectly efficient security system already installed, and it doesn't need any improvements.'

'I don't think that was what your father had in mind, Miss Davies.' The quiet voice mocked her deliberate, stiff formality. 'I take it you *are* Catherine?' he added with disturbing abruptness.

Taken by surprise, she swung round to face him. 'Of course I am. Who else did you think I could be?'

'A girlfriend?'

'My father's? Hardly! You can't know him very well if you'd think that.'

The strong shoulders under the perfectly fitted jacket lifted in a nonchalant shrug.

'You could have been. Or a nanny?' A faint grin surfaced at her look of frank disbelief. 'I never expected Lloyd's daughter to be so—mature...'

The last word was loaded with so much deliberate irony that it had a rush of hot colour flooding into her pale cheeks, all the more so because it was accompanied by

another of those insolent, assessing surveys, the cool
scrutiny searing over the pale oval of her face, with its
high cheekbones and full, rather wide mouth, before
moving slowly down the length of her body, lingering at
the soft swell of her breasts, the curves of her hips in
the worn denim jeans.

He might just as well have added the word 'physically' to that 'mature'—as it was, it seemed to hang in
the air between them, making Catherine's skin prickle
in irritation.

'After all, your father isn't exactly the sort of man
one would expect to have such a grown-up daughter—'

'My misspent youth catching up with me,' Lloyd put
in from the doorway, his laughter holding a trace of embarrassment. 'I was barely nineteen when Cathy was
born, though her mother was older—almost twenty-
four—'

'Really, Dad,' Catherine cut in hastily, 'Mr Lindsay
doesn't want to hear all the details of our family history.'

'On the contrary,' Evan corrected smilingly. 'I have
to admit to being rather intrigued. I came here expecting
to see someone who was perhaps six at the most, possibly
even younger. Instead, I'm confronted by a glamorous
blonde who is clearly not even an adolescent.'

'I'm twenty-six, if that's what you're angling to find
out.'

Catherine regretted the sharpness of her tone when
she saw the way those sea-toned eyes turned to her, their
regard coolly direct, clearly noting the raised colour in
her cheeks, the spark of reaction in her own bright blue
eyes. If that 'glamorous' had been meant to flatter, to
make her loosen up, then it had failed; if anything, she
felt even more uptight than before.

'I would have said twenty-two—no more,' Evan returned smoothly. 'But then the clothes are very deceptive—and without a trace of make-up you look like
a well-scrubbed young girl.'

'I don't like to wear make-up all the time. Having to—' She caught herself up sharply, not wanting to give too much away. 'I prefer to let my skin breathe,' she corrected hastily.

'My sister feels exactly the same way.'

It was a bland reply, easily spoken, but she knew that she hadn't succeeded in distracting him completely from the way she had covered up what she had been about to say. The aquamarine eyes had narrowed sharply, and she could sense a watchful awareness about the powerful body before her that made her stomach twist in painful apprehension.

Her father never seemed to dominate the room in quite the same way, she reflected nervously. He never made her feel that the elegant blue and grey room was somehow too small to contain him—or perhaps that was just a reflection of her own inner feelings, the tension that now always seemed to torment her when she was in the presence of any man she didn't know.

'That coffee must be ready by now. I'll go and get it.'

'Mrs Bentley will bring it through.'

'No.' She shook her head determinedly. 'I'll go and fetch it. You rely too much on your housekeeper since I left home, Dad. It's well after six, and she should have the rest of the evening off.'

She prayed that the words wouldn't sound like the excuse they were as she hastily made her way from the room, grateful for the chance to escape from Evan Lindsay, whose presence in her father's house had started to become distinctly unnerving, his watchful scrutiny disturbingly oppressive.

In the kitchen, her father's efficient housekeeper had everything ready, but all the same, after she had dismissed the older woman, Catherine lingered needlessly—rearranging the layout of the cups and saucers on the tray, adding a plate of biscuits, some hot milk as well as the cream, and finally coming to a halt, staring sightlessly at the bright floral blind that concealed the window as she had to face the fact that she was trying to avoid going back to join her father and his companion.

Was her nervousness just a natural response to events? she couldn't help wondering. Was it just the sort of fear that anyone else might experience if they had been subjected to the sort of pressures, the harassment that she had endured, or was it something more? Was it something more personal, more directly involved with Evan Lindsay himself?

She had acknowledged that shivering sense of reaction when she'd looked at him, the intuitive recognition of a streak of something dangerous in him that had lifted the tiny hairs on the back of her neck in the instinctive reaction of a wary cat faced with a hostile intruder into its territory, but could she trust that? Did that sense of recognition come from her own inner turmoil or some other, more primitive response to his own individual aura?

'Can I carry something through for you?'

The voice sounded suddenly behind her, making her start violently and drop the spoon she had been holding, letting it fall from nerveless fingers to land on the tray with a clatter that sounded appallingly loud in the quiet of the early evening. Reacting purely spontaneously, she swung round sharply, blue eyes blazing furiously.

'What the hell do you think you're doing, sneaking up on me like that? How dare you invade my privacy in this way? I—'

'Hey!'

Evan's hands shot out, catching her flailing arms in a powerful grip, stilling their wild gesticulations.

'Calm down, lady! There's no need for this.'

'No need!'

If he hadn't touched her then perhaps she might have been able to rein in her temper, get a grip on her self-control, but with the pressure of those strong fingers on her skin, sending electrical impulses shooting through every nerve, it seemed as if something had exploded inside her head, threatening to blow off the top of her skull.

Her vision hazed and she didn't see Evan Lindsay as a man but as the personification of the male force—big and dark and ominously threatening.

'No need! You creep in here—'

'I said, *calm down*!'

He actually shook her—not hard, but firmly enough to drive the message home, sweeping the panic from her mind and replacing it with a calmer, more logical way of thinking.

'You were a long time getting the coffee, and your father seemed concerned so I came to see if you needed any help. I wasn't creeping around anywhere!' he added more emphatically. 'It isn't my fault if you were so lost in a dream world that you didn't hear me come into the room.'

If she needed bringing back down to reality, then the look in those cold, sea-coloured eyes was enough to do just that. It was like having a bucketful of icy water thrown straight into her face, and it shocked her out of her panic without a second's hesitation, leaving her gasping in reaction.

'I—I'm sorry,' she said stiffly. 'I was—thinking of something else.'

'Obviously,' was the sardonic response. 'And something none too pleasant from the looks of things. Just what—?'

But Catherine had remembered exactly what she had been thinking in the moment that he had come up behind her, and with that half-formed fear of him still shadowing her mind she wasn't prepared to reveal any of her innermost feelings to him.

'My thoughts are my own, Mr Lindsay,' she returned tartly. 'I'll thank you not to poke your nose in where it's not wanted.'

'Fine.' The single syllable was cold and curt, like the smile that he switched on and off as briefly as a flashing neon sign.

It was only when he let go of her hands that she realised he had still held them, the jarring abruptness of the movement as her arms fell to her sides aggravating her already disturbed state of mind. But she was totally unprepared for the devastating and bewildering sense of loss that ripped through her as cold air reached the spot where the warm strength of his hands had been only seconds before, so that it was all she could do to keep herself from crying out in distress.

'Would you like some help with the tray, or would that be an invasion of your precious privacy too?'

'What? Oh, no—'

Catherine struggled to regain some composure, feeling as if the tattered shreds of her self-control were fluttering wildly round her like the remains of some torn and ragged garment.

'Thanks—that would be kind...'

Her voice faded as Evan moved forward, coming into the full glare of the fluorescent light for the first time, his features being thrown into harsh relief as if someone had directed a spotlight full on to his face.

He was definitely *not* a pretty man, or even a handsome one, she reflected privately. That strongly carved bone-structure was too harsh, too forceful to be described in any such way. He was a very tough-looking man—a man whose face seemed to be carved out of hard, unpolished wood, all knots and angles and...

'What happened to your nose?' The question escaped before she had time to consider whether it was wise to show an interest in such a personal matter.

'My nose?' He looked as startled as she felt to hear the words on her lips. 'Oh—that.'

Strong brown fingers touched the definite bump that marred the straightness in the centre of his face.

'I broke it.'

'Obviously.' She echoed his own sardonic tone of moments before. 'Any fool can see that—but how did it happen?'

A grin curled the corners of his mouth, mocking her indignation.

'In the army—on a training exercise.'

The smile grew, became devastating in its megawatt brilliance.

'I had to climb a rope that I believed had been fastened securely—it hadn't, and I fell—hard. Result—one broken nose and a badly bruised ego. Needless to say, I never trust myself to anything without double-checking now.'

'You were in the army? When? For how long?'

'A couple of years. I went in straight from school. My father felt I needed the discipline, and at the time I would have done anything to get away from home. It didn't last long, though,' he added drily. 'Let's say that the army and I didn't exactly—suit one another.'

Catherine could well believe it. Even from the little she had seen of Evan she had gained an impression of someone who was too much his own man to submit willingly to the sort of unquestioning routine that was part of army life.

'And I suppose that's where you learned about security techniques—I understand that a lot of ex-army men go into that sort of job.'

'The ones who don't become night-watchmen or *bodyguards*.'

He was deliberately probing now; she knew that from the laser-like intensity with which those changeable eyes were fixed on her face. He was echoing her own comment earlier, wanting to push her into explaining.

'We'd better get this coffee through to the lounge before it gets cold,' she said, carefully ignoring his pushing. 'Dad will be sending out a search-party for me.'

'Is he always this over-protective?'

The question came deceptively casually, with Evan's head turned away as he picked up the tray, but it was enough to stop her dead in her tracks, halfway towards the door.

'What do you mean, "over-protective"?' Her voice was pitched too high and she struggled to lower it a degree or two. 'He's just a normal, caring parent—'

'Sure . . .' Evan's tone poured scorn on her indignation. 'Look, honey, I don't normally jump to conclusions about people, but you two don't exactly have a run of the mill sort of relationship.'

'I don't know what you mean—'

'No? Then let me tell you about this afternoon. I've been working with your father for days, and for some time it's been obvious that his mind isn't exactly on his job. Then today I called in at his office to discuss some things I needed to talk over with him. He made it plain that I'd have to make it quick—that he couldn't be late home—and it wasn't long before I realised that he wasn't paying me any attention at all. In fact, his thoughts were miles away. In the end he just gave up pretending to listen and suggested that we continued our discussion at his home.'

'So what's wrong with that? Dad often brings work home if it's late.'

'It was barely five o'clock. His secretary hadn't even finished work for the day, but Lloyd Davies, the boss of the whole outfit, says he has to go home—he's worried about his daughter.'

The disturbing note in Evan's voice scraped over Catherine's exposed nerves, worsening their already raw sensitivity, and she found it impossible to meet that probing, searching gaze, concentrating instead on smoothing and folding a crumpled teatowel that lay on the draining-board, arranging it with over-meticulous care.

'Naturally, I assumed from his concern that his daughter was a young girl—school-age at most, maybe even younger—so you can imagine my surprise when I find she's not a child but a fully grown woman of twenty-six, someone well old enough—'

'My father and I are very close,' Catherine broke in on him, unable to face the prospect of the inevitable questions that she knew were coming. 'It's probably because the age-gap between us is so small.'

'It's more than that.'

'Are you implying—?'

'I'm implying nothing—just curious.'

'Look, my mother left when I was barely five, and Dad and I have been together ever since. Naturally, we're very close—very dependent—though I don't suppose you'd understand that.'

'And just what is that supposed to mean?' The very quietness of Evan's words was ominous, sending a shiver of apprehension down Catherine's spine.

'Well, you said you'd joined the army to get away from home. Just because you and your parents—or at least your father—didn't get on it doesn't mean you can judge my relationship with Dad by the same standards.'

That was definitely below the belt, she admitted privately, but refused to let herself feel guilty. After all, he had only himself to blame—he had started this line of questioning.

'And now, if you don't mind, I think we've delayed long enough. I'd like to drink my coffee before it's completely stone-cold—even if you wouldn't.'

And, not giving him a chance to say any more, she turned on her heel and marched off down the hall, not daring to look back to see the effect her words had had on him.

She had left him with no option but to follow, but she was pretty certain that Evan Lindsay was not the sort of man to let things rest. And from the expression on his face as he set the tray down on the coffee-table in the lounge she was worryingly aware of the fact that, far from appeasing his curiosity, she had in fact only stirred it further.

Privately she cursed her own nervousness, the tension that had driven her to overreact, responding to his questions in a way that had fuelled his interest, fanning it from a slowly smouldering ember to a brightly burning flame that would not easily be extinguished. Her stomach twisted itself into tight, painful knots of apprehension, anticipating with a terrible sense of inevitability the interrogation that she was sure must come.

She didn't have to wait long. She had barely had time to pour the coffee and hand a cup to Evan, serving him, as their guest, first, as courtesy demanded, before the moment she had dreaded arrived.

Leaning back in his chair with a deceptively convincing display of relaxed ease, he sipped at his drink, his expression thoughtful, then he turned those turquoise eyes on her face once more, the look in them alerting her to what was to come.

'It's been a beautiful week hasn't it?' he asked easily, and, taken completely by surprise because she had been expecting something else entirely, Catherine could only manage an inarticulate murmur that might have been agreement.

Her father, however, apparently oblivious to the dark, swirling undercurrents she sensed, nodded enthusiastically.

'Summer's finally here, it seems—and not before time. Last month was so wet and miserable—hardly flaming June! But it's certainly making up for it now.'

'So it seems.'

Catherine knew that she was actually gaping in confusion. She couldn't believe her ears. Surely Evan didn't actually intend to conduct a conversation about the *weather*?

'And, of course, the light evenings are a real bonus.'

'They certainly are.' The darkly sardonic intonation in Evan's voice grated on Catherine's raw nerves.

'Dad—'

Belatedly she had caught on to the path Evan was following, the way his mind was working, and she tried to inject a note of warning into the single word, signalling to her father with her eyes as she did so. But Lloyd seemed oblivious to her concern.

'Would you like a biscuit, Mr Lindsay?' she asked, the words hissing from between clenched teeth as she turned a fulminating glare on him.

'No thanks,' he returned blithely. 'But I would like an explanation.'

'An explanation?' Catherine's father frowned his lack of comprehension.

'Mr Lindsay seems to think that we're hiding something, Dad. Either that or we're quite unnatural simply because we happen to care about each other.'

'But, Cathy, don't you think—?'

'No!' With difficulty she stopped herself from screaming the word at him. 'I don't think we should give Mr Lindsay an explanation of *anything*—not that there is anything to explain . . .' She covered herself hastily and clumsily in nervous response to the gleam of triumph that lit up in Evan's eyes. 'And even if there was, then it's none of his business.'

'Ah, but that's where you're wrong,' Evan inserted blandly, setting down his coffee-cup and leaning forward to emphasise his point. 'You see, I think your father made it my business when he invited me here on the pretext of discussing matters that could easily have waited until tomorrow.'

'Made what your business?' Catherine made one last attempt at pretending that nothing was wrong.

'I don't know yet, but I intend to find out. From the moment that I first set foot in this house, it's been obvious that something is very wrong.'

'Oh, come now, Mr Lindsay, surely you're exaggerating? There's nothing—'

'Nothing?'

One dark eyebrow lifted in an expression of mocking disbelief, and Catherine had the uncomfortable feeling that even though Evan hadn't moved from his chair he had, mentally at least, backed her into a very tight corner indeed.

'All right, we'll take things logically,' he said in a dangerously quiet voice. 'One—your father's been like a cat on hot bricks all afternoon—barely listening to a word I've said, and certainly not giving his work the concentration it deserved.

'Two—' he ticked off each point as he made it, using the outstretched fingers of his left hand '—he had to rush home to look after his daughter—at five p.m. A time when even a schoolgirl would be safe in the house—especially with the housekeeper there.

'But three—this daughter isn't a child, or even an adolescent—she's twenty-six, and someone who, by her own admission, normally has a place of her own.'

He didn't miss a trick, Catherine thought despairingly. He'd even picked up on the fact that she had her own flat. It was no wonder that they hadn't been able to hide anything from him. Oh, why had her father had to bring this particular man home?

'Shall I go on?'

When Catherine and her father could only stare at him, unable to find a word to say, Evan nodded silently, his mouth tightening ominously.

'All right—so you have your own home, but for some reason you're hiding out at your father's—'

'I'm not hiding!'

'No?'

Once more that raised eyebrow questioned the truth of her outburst.

'Then why did your father feel it necessary to ring the bell—the bell to his own front door—when he arrived? And why did he call out as soon as he came in, if not to reassure you? Why do you jump like a scalded cat at the slightest sound, any unexpected movement?'

Catherine began to feel as if the quickfire questions were in fact blows to her head, making her reel sickeningly.

'Why did you turn on me as if I was an intruder from an alien planet when I came up behind you in the kitchen? And—last but not least—why, when it's the hottest week we've had all summer, when the temperatures have finally reached into the twenties and the rest of the country is enjoying the long, warm evenings— gardening, having barbecues, or simply sitting outside soaking up the sun—do you have every single curtain in every damn room pulled so tightly closed that a beam of light couldn't get through if it tried?

'Either one of you is a vampire and will shrivel up in the heat of the sun, or there's some other, more disturbing reason for this obsession with privacy.'

He stopped at last, looking straight at both of them in much the same way that the counsel for the prosecution would survey the accused, Catherine reflected miserably, knowing that there was no way she could deny his assessment of events. His case was watertight—and he knew it.

'So now,' Evan continued more slowly, sea-green eyes fixed on her face in a way that made her feel worryingly certain that he could see right through her head and read everything that was in her mind, 'are you going to stop playing silly games and tell me just what all this is about?'

CHAPTER TWO

'WELL?'

The single, harsh syllable fell into the stunned silence that was the only response Catherine and her father could make to the clear and terrifyingly accurate assessment of the situation he had just given them. There really wasn't any way they could possibly argue against it, she reflected unhappily.

'Well?' he repeated, more emphatically this time.

'I—don't know what you're talking about.'

Stubbornly Catherine clung to her determination not to reveal anything to him.

'You must have a very vivid imagination,' she went on, with a touch of airiness that didn't quite come off, instead making her sound brittle and highly-strung instead of achieving the insouciance she had aimed for. 'You seem to have cobbled together some sort of fantasy scenario out of a lot of perfectly ordinary facts...'

Her voice failed her as Evan, not bothering to answer her verbally, turned on her the sort of cold, contemptuous look from those aquamarine eyes that made her quail fearfully inside, wanting to curl her arms round her to protect herself. Her earlier impression had been right, she told herself on a wave of unease. If provoked, Evan Lindsay could be a very dangerous character indeed.

'It's no good Cathy.' Lloyd Davies pushed a hand through hair that was just a couple of shades darker than his daughter's. 'We can't keep pretending that nothing's wrong—'

'Dad!'

'We have to tell *someone*.' Her father ignored the reproachful glance she turned on him. 'And it strikes me that Evan is the sort of man who might be able to help. That's why—'

'I don't think anyone can help!' The tension that Catherine had been holding in check all evening finally got the better of her, and the words escaped in a despairing rush. 'Even the police—'

She cut herself off sharply, swallowing down what she had been about to say as Evan's reaction told her just how much she had given away. The relaxed, almost indolent pose vanished as he sat up straight in his chair, his blue-green eyes fixed on her face.

'The *police*?'

Catherine's heart lurched painfully in her chest, every trace of confidence burned away in the cold fire of those changeable eyes, and she could only nod silently, her tongue seeming to have frozen in her mouth.

'Why are the police involved in this?'

If he had stayed where he was then perhaps she might have been able to answer him, but to Catherine's shock and total consternation Evan got up from his seat and came towards her, leaning down to rest both hands on the arms of her chair as he looked deep into her face.

'Catherine?'

God, she hadn't realised just how big a man he was— big and imposing and frighteningly strong. He was tough too; the set of his features told her that—the hard, square jaw, the tightness of the muscles around his mouth, the fierce, unblinking stare of those eyes.

A few moments earlier she had wondered what he would be like with the calm, affable veneer he had shown them up to now stripped away and the real Evan Lindsay revealed underneath. Now she was beginning to get some idea of the reality. The civilised finish had worn a little thin, exposing glimpses of a very different man—a man who was very much a force to be reckoned with.

'Evan—I—' her father began, but Evan let him get no further, cutting him off sharply.

'I'm talking to your daughter,' he flung over his shoulder, sparing the older man only the briefest of glances before turning his attention back to Catherine. '*Why* are the police involved in all this?'

Catherine struggled for some degree of control, her eyes wide and brilliant as sapphires over pale, drawn cheeks as she fought against the panic that was welling up inside her, threatening to take control. Earlier she had been fearful of Evan simply because he was a man, one she didn't know, but now it was more personal, more specific to him. She recalled how he had told her that he had been in the army, and her imagination conjured up images of all the interrogation scenes in any film she had ever seen, making her shiver in apprehension.

'You're frightening me!' she managed on a shaky gasp.

Evan's response was immediate and unexpected. His head went back sharply, his eyes darkening in something close to shock, and he looked down at his hands, realising the aggressive nature of his position, the implied threat in the way he towered over her.

'I'm sorry!' he said abruptly, moving back swiftly and raking one hand through the ebony sleekness of his hair in a gesture that spoke more clearly of his mental disturbance than any words could ever do. 'I'm sorry,' he repeated, his voice rough and slightly husky. 'I didn't mean to upset you.'

Catherine was shocked to find that his features seemed blurred, that tears had filled her eyes, obscuring her vision, and she blinked hard to try to clear them away.

'I'd like you to go now.' But even as she spoke the words she knew that she had little hope that Evan would do as she asked.

'Oh, no.'

The hard voice confirmed her fears, the adamant shake of his dark head driving home the point without hope of reprieve.

'You've involved me now. I'm not leaving until you tell me just what's going on.'

'But you have an appointment.'

It was a last ditch effort, the only card she had to play, and the desperation in her voice revealed how close she was to breaking.

Her hopes rose slightly when Evan looked at his watch and frowned in response to her words. An hour, he had said, and most of that time was already gone.

Catherine could hardly believe her eyes when he turned on his heel and headed for the door. Surely it couldn't be all over; it couldn't be that easy!

It wasn't. In the hall she heard Evan come to a halt, and then the sound of the telephone receiver being picked up. Without so much as a by your leave he pressed the number buttons with firm decisiveness.

'Sam?' His voice carried clearly to where she sat. 'About tonight—I'm afraid something's come up and I'm not going to be able to make it. Can we arrange another time?'

This Samantha must be an amazingly tolerant woman, Catherine reflected. There had been no apology, no hint of contrition in Evan's voice, only that laconic 'Something's come up.' Or was it *Samuel*, and so a very different matter entirely?

'Cathy, I think we have to tell him.' Her father's tone was urgent, pushing her to agree. 'You need someone—'

'Someone, yes—but not Evan Lindsay.'

'But why not? It's his line—his territory, so to speak.'

'But we don't know anything about him.'

Catherine couldn't put into words the way she felt, the fear that the thought of venturing into Evan Lindsay's 'territory' aroused in her. It smacked of

stepping blindfolded into the lion's den, if not precisely
putting her head in its mouth.

'We don't know who he is—what he is.'

'Fine.' In the hallway, Evan was bringing his conversation to an end. 'I'll see you then.'

'I know he's very good at his job—came highly re-
commended—and he's certainly been more than
thorough. And you know that I can't be here after this
week—'

'But I can.'

Catherine's head jerked up, her gaze going to the
doorway in nervous response to Evan's low-toned interjection. Still standing just outside the room, he studied
her for a long, taut moment, blue-green eyes narrowed,
his expression thoughtful.

'You weren't joking about the bodyguard,' he pronounced at last, making Catherine draw in her breath
sharply, wondering how she had ever hoped to hide anything from this perceptive, keenly observant man. 'Don't
you think you'd better let me in on the secret? At least
that way I'll be on your side.'

'Cathy,' Lloyd prompted, 'please...'

'I—don't know.' Her blue eyes were shadowed and
dull, looking faintly bruised above the colourless skin
of her cheeks. 'I don't even know if you could help.'

Evan moved suddenly, coming to sit opposite her once
more, his eyes holding hers all the time. Leaning forward,
he took her hands in both of his, his grip warm and
firm, the intensity of his gaze seeming to have the power
to draw her soul right out of her body.

'Try me,' he said softly.

In that moment something happened—something
strange and wonderful and totally inexplicable. In the
second that he spoke the quiet words it was suddenly as
if a huge weight had fallen from Catherine's heart, as
if all her doubts and fears had been taken from her,
washed away on a new tide of hope and fresh confidence.

Here was a pair of strong shoulders onto which she could shift the burden that had blighted her days; here was a calm, intelligent mind that could find a way through the waking nightmare that her life seemed to have become. She no longer had doubts, no longer needed to hesitate, to be wary.

'Help me,' she said simply, and saw his eyes darken, saw the stunning gentleness of his smile.

It would be easy to fall in love with a man with eyes like that, whose mouth could curve in that way, lighting up his whole face, she thought dreamily, allowing the fantasy to take root for a brief, delirious second, before the realisation of the foolhardy direction of her thoughts had her blinking in sudden shock.

'If I can, I will.' Evan's response was low and firm, the conviction in his voice enough to inspire confidence in even the most craven of hearts. 'But first you have to help me. I need to know just what's troubling you,' he added when he saw her puzzled frown. 'Do you trust me enough to tell me?'

Did she? Could she trust him? Who else could she turn to if she didn't tell him? There was no one else; it was Evan or no one.

'I don't know where to begin...' She had kept it to herself for so long that now it was difficult actually to let it out.

'Is it a man?' Evan prompted when she hesitated, shaking her head in despair.

'Yes—at least, I think so. Oh, but not in the way you mean. I'm sorry—I'm not doing this very well.'

Evan's silent shrug dismissed her apology as unnecessary.

'Take your time. We have all night.'

Now we have, Catherine thought, recalling the way he had dismissed the waiting Sam. But there was something very reassuring about that 'we'.

'Perhaps a drink would help—something stronger than coffee,' Lloyd put in, getting to his feet and heading towards the drinks cabinet.

'I think not.' Evan's incisive command stopped him halfway. 'We'd do better with clear heads—don't you think?'

Those last three words were added purely for courtesy's sake, Catherine realised. Evan's words had had the force of an order, one he intended to be obeyed without argument, and her father had recognised that, sinking back into his chair without a protest. For better or worse, Evan Lindsay was now in charge. They had put themselves into his hands and there was no going back.

Into his hands—the words reverberated inside her head as she let her gaze drop to the fingers that still held her own, recognising their strength with a shiver of reaction that was a disturbing blend of relief and fear. She was painfully aware of the potential power in Evan's hands— the force that, if it tightened just a tiny bit more, could bruise or break. Right now, she could only be grateful for the fact that that strength would be on her side.

'I don't know what my father told you about me...'

It was as if that thought had given her a mental push, and suddenly the words came tumbling out, like water pouring through newly opened floodgates.

'But I work in television—children's programmes, actually—and a couple of years ago I got a really big break when I was chosen to host a regular weekly show. It's called *Get Up and Go*. I don't know if you've heard of it, but—'

But Evan was nodding. 'Tuesdays—five till six.'

'You know about it?'

'My friend's kids love it. They wouldn't miss it for the world. You have two very loyal fans there.'

'That's great. How old are they—your friend's children, that is?'

She spoke quickly, needing to distract herself from the sudden disturbing lurch her heart had given. When he smiled like that it lit up his whole face, softening the hard lines and making the blue-green eyes glow like a rock pool when the sun fell on it.

'Five and seven—a boy and a girl. Amy's the seven-year-old—she's the real fan.'

'Well, five is perhaps a little young to take it all in.'

She wouldn't allow herself to wonder whether the friend he had referred to was the same one he had spoken of earlier. Were these the children of the Sam he had been going to have dinner with? It was worrying to find that in spite of her attempts to drive it from her mind the answer to that question suddenly seemed very important.

'I always like to hear firsthand that people enjoy what we do. Of course, we do get a lot of letters—'

'But not all of them from kids.'

The faint shake in her voice had betrayed her; either that or some tiny reaction in her face that had not escaped those watchful aquamarine eyes.

'No.' Her voice was very low.

'And not all just expressing innocent admiration.' It was a statement, not a question.

'No.' She shook her head, grateful for the way the movement made her fair hair fly around her face, concealing the vulnerability of her expression.

'Cathy's been the victim of a campaign of harassment,' her father put in. 'A stalker, I believe the current word is—an obsessive fan.'

'An adult fan?' Evan's attention was concentrated on Catherine. 'When did all this start?'

'About seven months ago; just before Christmas. The first letter came in a bundle of ordinary mail, and really it was just very complimentary about my appearance.' Catherine's laugh was shaken. 'He said I was just what he wanted in his Christmas stocking. But there was a tone to it—some rather sexual comments that made it plain it didn't come from a typical fan. Your friend's daughter and son are the sort who usually write.'

'It was anonymous, I take it?'

'Yes. There was another one the next week, and the next, and every week after that—sometimes two or three in a row. They started off mild enough, but they soon got more and more sexually explicit—more expressive of his personal fantasies—more disgusting.' She shuddered, remembering.

'But they just came to the television studios?'

'No. I think I could have coped with that, but after a month or so they started arriving at my flat. He'd got my address from somewhere—where, I don't know. And the letters were just the beginning. The next thing that happened was the parcels—'

'Parcels?'

Catherine nodded miserably.

'They contained underwear mostly—stockings, suspenders, G-strings. He'd write that he wanted to see me in them.' She tried another laugh, one that broke up in the middle. 'He must have spent a fortune.'

But Evan wasn't laughing. As she'd told her story his expression had grown grimmer, darker, more dangerous—so that, looking at him, she could barely suppress a shiver of fearful reaction.

'Go on,' he prompted harshly when she hesitated. 'I take it there was more?'

'That was only the beginning...'

Now she wanted everything out in the open, wanted to pour the whole story out, as if by doing so she could purge herself of the horror, the fear with which she had lived for so long. So she told him how the letters had grown more and more sexually threatening, how the unknown stalker had declared that he believed she was his destiny, that one day they were meant to be together.

'He even started to interpret things I'd said on the programme—things I'd said to children—as being messages just for him.'

Once again she shuddered, her blue eyes dark and shadowed.

'He referred to them in his letters, giving them totally different meanings—making them disgusting and dirty. That was when we called the police, but of course there was no real evidence.'

'The letters?'

Sadly, Catherine shook her head.

'I burned most of them. Oh, I know I shouldn't have done, but at first I just didn't think it would last—I thought he'd soon get tired of pestering me. And then, later, they were so horrible that I couldn't bear to have them around, and I destroyed them without thinking that they would be needed. Once I'd told the police they said I should pass the letters on to them unopened.'

'Good advice,' Evan put in quietly. 'Did that help?'

'I wish I could say it had; if anything, it made matters worse. It was as if he knew what I'd done and he changed his routine as a result. That was when the phone calls started.'

Evan muttered something violent and obscene in a savage undertone, drawing her pansy-dark eyes to his face. Seeing the cold fury etched around his nose and mouth, she hesitated, almost fearful of continuing. Immediately he made himself relax, wiping the harsh lines from his face with a speed that made her blink.

'Go on,' he encouraged with an unexpected softness, warm fingers tightening slightly on hers.

'He started ringing me at my flat—sometimes in the evening, just after I'd got home from work, sometimes in the middle of the night.'

'Did you recognise the voice?' The question came sharply.

'No—but I think he'd done something to disguise it—put a handkerchief over the mouthpiece or something—and he always whispered, so that distorted it too. He seemed to be getting more obsessed—more angry. There was one time when he'd seen me on the show with another presenter. He thought I'd been flirting—''unfaithful'' he called it! He said I was a two-timing bitch and if I didn't change my ways he would punish me—'

Her breath caught in her throat, threatening to choke her, and she had to pause, struggling to control the panic that rose up in her. Evan waited silently, seeming to sense intuitively that to speak would be to destroy her composure completely, but those strong, warm fingers still intertwined with hers tightened in an eloquent communication of sympathy.

'I'd had an answering machine installed, but I found that I was just standing by it, waiting to hear his voice, and he always seemed to know when I was there. He said that he'd make sure I never had a relationship with anyone else—he'd kill anyone I dated—and—and if necessary he'd kill me.'

Her voice broke again, her eyes flooding with tears, but it was as if Evan was passing his strength on to her through his touch on her hands, and in a moment she was able to continue.

'The police did what they could. They tried to trace the calls, but they were all from payphones scattered all over London. They even offered to escort me to and from work, but I couldn't take that—it was like being a prisoner—and I couldn't rest in my flat, never knowing when the phone might ring again, whether it would be him... It all came to a head last week when I was out shopping. I'd just gone to the supermarket to get some groceries, but suddenly I heard someone running behind me.'

Once more she shuddered, reliving the fear she had felt in that moment.

'It was only a man running for a bus, but it panicked me. I realised that he could be watching me all the time— following me. I just snapped. I came straight here, didn't even go home to get any clothes. I was afraid he might be there waiting for me.'

Abruptly Catherine became aware of the fact that she was still holding onto Evan's hands, her fingers clenched on his, tightening in response to her inner distress, and with a muffled exclamation she released them sharply, her confusion growing as she saw the red marks on his skin, the indentations where her nails had dug into his palms.

'Oh, I'm sorry!' She couldn't believe her own thoughtlessness.

Evan barely spared his hands the briefest of glances, his shrug dismissing both the damage she had done and her apology.

'And what's happened since you came here? Have things been easier?'

'Oh, yes. Only one person knows where I am and that's my agent. I had to tell her, because she's a special friend as well as working with me. And I rang work and told them I was ill—exhaustion due to stress. Well, it's near enough to the truth. Luckily, we've just finished filming the last of the current series, so I'm not leaving anyone in the lurch—and I was due two months' leave anyway. They probably realise something's up; my mind hasn't exactly been on my job lately.'

'But what will happen when your leave is up? You can't hide away here for ever.'

'I know. I have to admit that I haven't really thought beyond that. I suppose I'm just praying that something will be resolved before I have to go back—that the police track him down, or he loses interest in tormenting me and gives up. I just know I can't bear the thought of him being out there—watching.'

'Are you sure you're not letting him win by giving in to him in this way—letting him ruin your life?'

'Oh, you would say that! You're a man!' Catherine couldn't believe she had actually trusted this man, poured her heart out to him, only to get this typical masculine response. 'You don't know what it's like to live in fear— not to feel secure in your own home—'

'It was a question that had to be asked.'

'Of course you'd see it that way.' Unable to bear that intent sea-coloured gaze any longer, she got to her feet in a restless, disturbed movement. 'I don't know why I ever told you.'

If she had expected that confiding in him would bring a sense of relief, then she had been desperately wrong. Instead, she felt even more vulnerable than before, frightened by the way she had let a complete stranger into the carefully restricted, protective world that had enclosed her safely until now.

'You obviously can't or won't help me.'

'Did I say that?'

It was his very stillness that shook her, making her stop dead in the middle of the room. Evan hadn't moved an inch; he still sat in his chair, his hands lying loosely on its arms, his hard-boned face turned towards her. He was so big that even sitting down he didn't have to tilt his head much to look up at her.

'Don't put words into my mouth, Catherine.' The ominous quietness of his tone was somehow more disturbing than if he had shouted, and it dried Catherine's mouth so that she had to swallow hard.

'I—' she began, not really knowing what she was going to say, but at that moment the shrill of the telephone slashed through her words. Immediately she froze, her eyes, dark with fear, going to her father.

'Dad—'

But Evan had already reacted. Getting up and out of his chair in one swift, lithe movement, he was in the hall and had snatched up the receiver before Catherine had even registered the action.

'Yes?' he snapped. 'Who do you want to speak to? Who shall I say? If you'd just hold the line a minute, please.'

'Please', Catherine noted, relief breaking over her like a fierce wave, so that she had to cling to a nearby chair for support. Obviously *not* anyone she should fear, then. The release from the tension that held her prisoner every day was so intense that she felt tears prick at her eyes.

'Catherine?' Evan had his finger on the secrecy button of the phone. 'Do you want to speak to someone called Ellie?'

'Oh, yes.' The strength returned to her legs at the sound of the familiar name. 'It's my agent,' she explained, taking the telephone from his hand, expecting that he would move away, at least to a discreet distance. But instead he lingered, leaning back against the wall, his arms folded. 'Ellie—is that you?' She forced herself to ignore him.

'None other,' her friend's voice said clearly on the other end of the line, and Catherine smiled to herself, picturing the older woman's smiling face, her once bright red hair, now fading to a sort of pepper-and-salt effect. 'Though I'm not sure I dare speak to you after that cross-examination. Just who is the pit bull, and is he as terrifying as he sounds?'

'The—? Oh—yes.'

As light dawned as to just what Ellie was talking about, Catherine couldn't resist a swift, laughing glance across at where Evan stood, still very much on the alert.

'Yes, he is,' she managed, wondering if he had heard himself described as a guard dog.

'All ripping teeth and vicious snarl?'

'Hardly!' This time her amused eyes met those watchful turquoise ones. 'This is a private phone call,

Evan,' she added with a pointed glance at the door into the lounge.

She might have spared herself the effort. Evan simply ignored her reaction, returning her look with disturbing lack of reaction, all emotion blanked out as if he hadn't heard a word, and settled himself more firmly against the wall.

'Evan, eh?' Ellie had heard her aside. 'So who might he be? Anyone interesting?'

'Not at all.' Furious at Evan's deliberate rudeness, Catherine no longer cared what he heard, and she deliberately turned her back on him. 'He's just some security man who works for my father.'

'And now for you, is that it? Are you finally seeing sense and hiring yourself a bodyguard? About time, too. So tell me—' a hint of wicked humour lit Ellie's voice '—what's he like? I mean, we've all seen the film . . .'

'Forget it, Ellie!' The knowledge that Evan was still there, a silent observer of her every move, provoked some imp of mischief in her to add, 'This guy's no Kevin Costner—you were closer with the pit bull terrier.'

'All brawn and no brain, huh?' Ellie didn't sound too disappointed. 'Oh, well, that type's good for other things, I suppose. I mean, if you can't enjoy his conversation, at least you can enjoy something else . . .'

'Ellie!' As her friend's salacious laugh made it plain exactly what she meant, Catherine struggled to resist the urge to look over her shoulder and see how Evan had taken that comment. 'No one would believe you were a respectable, mature married lady. Anyway, it's not like that.'

'Not your type?'

'Definitely not.' The sudden prick of her conscience, reminding her of the sensual awareness she had felt while alone with Evan in the kitchen and at other points of the evening, gave Catherine's tone an unwarranted decisiveness. 'Besides, I'm definitely off men at the moment, after all that's happened.'

'Of course you are, love.' Ellie's tone had sobered. 'It must be hell to feel so hunted. That's why I rang, to find out how things are on that front. Any news?'

'If you mean do the police have any leads, then the answer's no. And I daren't go back to my flat—I reckon I'll— Hey!'

She broke off on a cry that was a mixture of nervous reaction and outraged fury as there was a sudden movement from behind her and Evan's strong finger came down hard on the disconnect button, cutting her off abruptly.

'What the hell did you do that for?' Blue eyes blazing, she swung round to face him. 'Just what do you think you were doing?'

'Stopping you from giving too much away,' was the imperturbable reply.

'But Ellie's my friend, for God's sake! She wouldn't—'

'No? Can you be sure of that?'

'Of course I can. I've known her almost all my life; she was like a mother to me when mine walked out. She wouldn't—you can't think that!'

'All I know is that you were about to tell her exactly what your plans are, and as far as I'm concerned the fewer people who know, the better. You did ask me to help,' he pointed out, with an infuriatingly exaggerated reasonableness that set Catherine's teeth on edge.

'But not in this arrogant manner!' Ruthlessly Catherine ignored the memory of her own voice pleading, 'Help me,' a short time before. 'Ellie is my *friend*!'

'In that case she'll understand. And if nothing else, your friend has a very loud mouth. If you want my opinion.'

'I don't think I do!'

Catherine slammed the phone back down onto its rest and, turning on her heel, stalked back into the lounge, her head high. Right now, she felt that having to put up with Evan Lindsay's high-handed behaviour was too high a price to pay even for protection from the menace of the stalker. In a moment of weakness she had turned to him, but that didn't mean she wanted him to move in and take over her life!

'I don't want your opinion, or your help—or anything!'

'But, Cathy—' Her father's concerned face showed his worried response to her outburst. 'What will you do next week?'

'Precisely what happens then?' Evan asked from the doorway.

'I have to go to Japan.' Lloyd ignored his daughter's furious glare, the message not to answer that she was trying to telegraph with her eyes. 'I'll be away for nearly a month. I don't want to leave Cathy on her own.'

'I can cope—'

'Oh, sure.' Evan's tone was rich with sardonic disbelief. 'You can *cope* the way you were doing before tonight—jumping at your own shadow, frightened by the least sound, imprisoned in—'

'I'll be *fine!*'

She would be, just to spite him. Give this man an inch and he took five hundred miles. She didn't want him trampling all over her life with his great size elevens, putting his nose in where it wasn't wanted, cutting her off from her friends.

'I've changed my mind. I don't want anything—'

Once more she was silenced by the sound of the telephone. Ellie, she thought, ringing back to find out just what had happened before. She actually had her hand on the receiver when it was wrenched away from her.

'Yes?' Even curter than before, if that was possible.

'How dare you? It's only Ellie—'

She was reaching out to snatch the phone back when she saw his expression change, the hardening of those strongly carved features, the cold light that came into his eyes, and a sensation like the shiver of icy water slid slowly down her spine.

'There's no one called Honey here.'

Honey. It was all she could do to suppress a moan of terror. The sound of the name had the force of a blow to her head, filling her mouth with a taste that was bitter as acid.

Honey. That was *his* name for her—the name he had written at the beginning of each letter, and, more recently, the way he always started each hateful, horrible phone call. She could hear it now inside her head, that terrible, terrifying whisper—'Hello, Honey.'

Every trace of colour drained form her cheeks, leaving them white and ashen, and she took a shaky step backwards.

At once Evan's gaze went to her face, aquamarine eyes narrowing swiftly as he took in her reaction. His response was immediate, no questions needing to be asked.

'There's no Honey here, and there never will be again—not for you. Do you understand that? No, *you* can listen! You're not dealing with Honey now; you're dealing with me. No, it doesn't matter who the hell I am. All you need to know is that I'm here, and I'm in charge, and I don't take too kindly to—'

He broke off sharply, listening intently to whatever the person on the other end of the line was saying. To Catherine's shock and consternation his response was laughter, but laughter that was so terrifyingly hard and humourless that it worried her almost as much as the knowledge that her tormentor had tracked her down once more.

'Do that.' The brutal satisfaction in Evan's tone made Catherine's stomach clench painfully. 'And I'll derive a great deal of pleasure from taking you apart, limb by limb. What? Oh, no, pal, I won't be going anywhere. I'm staying right here, and I don't intend to leave until you're safely locked away. So if you want to get to your Honey, you'll have to come through me first!'

Then, as Catherine watched with the sort of trans-fixed fascination that a rabbit displayed when con-fronted by a predatory snake, he grinned suddenly, with grim triumph, and let the phone drop onto the table with a clatter that to her overwrought nerves seemed as loud as thunder overhead.

'He's gone,' he said, that dark satisfaction still lin-gering in his words. 'He's a man of limited vocabulary, isn't he, your Joe?'

And if she had any doubts as to who the caller had been then that drove them away. Honey was what he called her; Joe was his name for himself. Joe as in Joe Public—ordinary Joe. She had no doubt that it was not his real name.

'Oh, God!' Her hand went to her mouth, her eyes deep pools of fear above her concealing fingers. 'What am I going to do?'

'Do?' To her consternation, Evan smiled with sudden, disturbing gentleness. '*You* don't have to do anything.'

'But—'

'But nothing. Didn't you hear what I said? I'll handle things from here on in. I'm in charge now.'

If it was meant to reassure, then his harsh declaration didn't have the desired effect. In Catherine's mind there was not all that much to choose between Evan Lindsay and the stalker who was hounding her. And she couldn't help wondering just what sort of a force she had un-leashed by getting this man involved in her situation—in her life.

CHAPTER THREE

CATHERINE woke the next morning to a terrible sense of foreboding, and a feeling of having burned her boats, aggravating rather than improving her situation—which was all the more illogical when she considered that all she had actually done was enlist someone to help her. She should have felt more relaxed, a burden shared was a burden halved, they said, but that was very far from the case.

'What have we done, Dad?' she asked when, with her face pale after a disturbed night, she joined her father at the breakfast table. 'Is Evan really the man we want?'

'Of course he is, darling.' Lloyd lifted puzzled eyes from his newspaper. 'He's a security expert—one of the top men in his field.'

'Yes, but he's so—*tough*.'

Recalling Evan's behaviour on the previous night, Catherine couldn't suppress a faint shudder at the thought of the hard-faced determination with which he had ignored her request for privacy, the controlled force behind his action as he'd cut off the phone call from Ellie, the ruthless, cold ferocity that had been in his face and his voice when he had spoken to Joe.

'Don't you think we need someone tough? Look, Cathy, this stalker is ruining your life, making each day a misery. You have to be protected from that, and to my mind it's time he got some of his own medicine—time we started fighting fire with fire.'

'But that's just what I'm afraid of. Isn't fighting fire with fire more likely to end up causing a raging inferno rather than actually extinguishing anything? After all,

41

what do we know about this Evan Lindsay, other than that he's some sort of security man?'

'Personally, nothing at all. But he's more than just a security man. As I said, he's an expert, and the company he set up has won a worldwide reputation and respect. He doesn't do this for the money, Cathy—he doesn't need to.'

'But I thought—' And she had referred to him as just a security man!

'That he was one of the workmen? Not Evan; he's the big boss. He could leave everything to the men he employs, but that's not his way. After all, he didn't have to check those things through with me last night—though I must say that that turned out for the best.'

So, did this new knowledge change her perception of Evan? Catherine wondered. It certainly went a long way towards explaining the aura of arrogant power and command that seemed to permeate every bone in his body. But money wasn't everything. He was still Evan Lindsay, who, apart from that arrogance and a total ruthlessness that had shown through the polite social veneer, was very much an unknown quantity.

'After all, if he hadn't suggested that he came back here with me then he wouldn't have been around when that phone call—'

'*Evan* suggested—but I thought he said that *you* invited him here.'

'You must have heard him wrong, darling. It was all his idea.'

The sound of a car door slamming in the drive outside brought Lloyd to his feet in a rush, twitching aside a bit of the curtain to peer through the crack. Catherine watched tensely, her fingers tightening on the handle of her cup.

'It's all right—it's Evan. Oh, come on, poppet—get rid of that glum face. He's on our side, remember.'

Which was supposed to make her feel a lot better, Catherine reflected worriedly as her father left the room in order to let Evan in at the front door, but somehow it had exactly the opposite effect. She couldn't quite put her finger on what was wrong. She knew she needed help—she had even, in a moment of weakness, turned to Evan and begged him to look after her—but that didn't mean that she was happy about him taking over her life in the way he had done last night.

'I'm in charge now,' he had said, and had proceeded to demonstrate precisely how strongly he meant that, moving into action with a speed and force that had made her feel as if she had been hit by a whirlwind. He had checked every aspect of the house and gardens with a thoroughness that even she had privately thought excessive, and issued a stream of instructions to herself and her father before he had finally departed, promising to be round as soon as possible the next day.

'But not this early!' Catherine said aloud, belatedly becoming aware of the fact that, with no appointments planned for the day ahead, she had come straight down to breakfast in her nightclothes, pausing only to pull on a white, short-sleeved broderie anglaise robe over the matching baby-doll-length nightdress. As a result, she was hardly suitably dressed to receive an unknown man as a visitor, and she certainly didn't want him getting the wrong impression.

Because that was where the problem lay. After all, Evan Lindsay was a stranger. He was every bit as unknown to her as the hateful tormentor who called himself Joe, and under normal circumstances there was no way she would have considered giving him a free rein in running her life.

'Come along in, Evan. I'm sure you could do with a cup of coffee.'

Her father clearly shared none of her doubts—but then why should he? she asked herself with a touch of asperity. As she had told Evan last night, no man—not even her beloved father—could understand fully how it felt to be persecuted in this way, to look at every man who passed and wonder, Is that him?

'It's Evan, darling,' Lloyd announced—quite unnecessarily as the younger man had preceded him into the room, seeming to fill it with his size and strength.

'Obviously,' Catherine muttered, embarrassment at her state of undress making her voice waspish. She hadn't even combed her hair, she now realised as that cool seagreen gaze swept over her in a swift, assessing survey, and its usual sleek elegance was roughly tousled, falling in pale, disordered waves around a face that was shadowed from lack of sleep.

'You're not dressed!' he said, not even bothering with a greeting, and she bridled at the sharpness of his tone.

'And good morning to you too!' she retorted, her earlier embarrassment evaporating in the heat of her flaring irritation.

Had she really been worried that Evan might read something she didn't mean into her state of undress? She couldn't have been more wrong. The cold fire of the look that had seared over her had held nothing sexual, or even anything that could be termed a response to her appearance. Instead, his eyes had blazed with an icy contempt that made her grit her teeth in fury.

'No, I'm not dressed—but then we didn't expect you to appear on our doorstep at the crack of dawn!'

She knew she sounded shrewish, but it was impossible to impose any degree of control on her voice because the anger that she felt had now combined with a sudden, unexpected sensual reaction that exploded in her mind, making her thoughts reel as she took in Evan's appearance properly for the first time. Gone was the tailored suit of the day before, and in its place was a black T-shirt and black jeans that clung to the powerful lines of his body in a way that made her mouth dry simply to see it.

This was not the businessman of the day before—the man whose restrained, formal clothing seemed to belie the force of the body beneath it, whose sleekly conservative outfit was very much at odds with the powerful, primitively potent masculinity he possessed. This man had a lethally attractive, devastatingly sexual impact that was like a blow straight to her stomach.

'I did say first thing.' Evan turned a pointed glance on the clock on the mantelpiece—a clock which showed the time as being only just past eight. 'I've been up for almost two hours.'

'And I suppose you've jogged twelve miles, done a hundred press-ups and eaten a perfectly low-fat, high-fibre breakfast—after you'd showered and shaved, of course.'

'Something like that.' A grin appeared briefly—so briefly that it was only when it had gone again that she realised how dramatically it had transformed his face, softening the hard lines and bringing a warm light to those aquamarine eyes. 'Actually, I swam this morning, but the rest of your guess was pretty accurate.'

'All right, so you're perfect, but you'll have to allow the rest of us mere mortals to be rather more humanly fallible. After all, I am usually up and on my way to work around this time, but circumstances are rather different these days—and this is my home.'

'Your father's home—in which you are currently hiding from a psychotic stalker who has threatened to harm you and anyone close to you,' Evan returned bluntly, the cold incisiveness of his tone making the words seem all the more frightening. 'Wouldn't it make more sense to be up and dressed, ready for any eventuality, rather than flaunting yourself in—'

'I am *not* "flaunting" myself!'

'No?'

Once more that changeable gaze swept over her, drawing hot blood into her cheeks and into the exposed skin of her arms and legs as it passed downwards, almost as if she had been exposed to the burning rays of the sun.

She might have been piqued earlier by the lack of interest in the way he looked at her, but that was no longer true of the scrutiny to which he subjected her now. There was no warmth in it at all, but nevertheless it was as blatantly sexual as any lascivious ogling she had ever endured, making her draw the fragile protection of her thin robe more closely around her—though she was well aware of the fact that there was so little of it that it had hardly any effect on the amount of her body that was exposed to those probing eyes.

'No?' Evan repeated, one eyebrow drifting upwards in sardonic mockery of her attempts at concealment. 'From where I'm standing, that scrap of material looks calculated to inflame any red-blooded man's erotic fantasies—and, believe me, that's just how Joe would see it.'

'Don't you think you're exaggerating the situation rather? I mean—'

'He knows where you're living now; he proved that last night. And this house is somewhat isolated. There's that long drive, with all the trees lining it—it would provide good cover for anyone who wanted to get up here without being seen. And although you've still got all the curtains drawn, there are plenty of cracks where they haven't joined properly. All he needs is a good telescope or a pair of binoculars and—'

'You've made your point! I'll get dressed.' Catherine got to her feet in a rush.

To his credit, Evan concealed any satisfaction he might have been feeling at her capitulation, simply nodding and settling himself in a chair at the breakfast table. He poured himself a cup of coffee before leaning back in his seat, very much at home.

'Wear something comfortable and practical,' he advised as she headed for the door. 'Jeans and a T-shirt—that sort of thing. Oh, and have you got your car keys somewhere?'

'Car keys?' Catherine turned in the doorway, looking back at him in confusion. 'Yes, they're in my room but—'

'Drop them down to me before you change. I'll get rid of your car while you're getting ready.'

'Get rid—! You'll do no such thing!' The little red sports car was her pride and joy—her key to freedom. 'Damn you, Evan—'

He ignored her outburst. 'That car's a dead giveaway—too distinctive by half. You might just as well put a sign on the gate—"Miss Catherine Davies is living here".'

He had a point—again.

'But he already knows that—he phoned here last night.'

'And you want him to know you're still here? Just as long as that car stays in the garage he knows you haven't moved on somewhere else. I'll take very good care of it,' he added cajolingly, with a smile that did disturbing things to Catherine's insides, reducing her determination not to give in to the liquid consistency of melted butter.

He might be an arrogant, domineering bastard, but when he softened his voice like that, and added a smile to match, it would be difficult to refuse him anything, she reflected. The problem was that she rather suspected that he knew that only too well—that the effect of his behaviour was calculated to the millimetre.

'I'll bring the keys down when I'm dressed,' she flung at him rebelliously, enjoying the flare of defiance as evidence of the fact that she wasn't as easily swayed as he might have thought.

Her sense of triumph didn't last long.

'I think it'd be better if I came up with you now to collect them. Best to get it done as soon as possible. In fact...'

He swallowed the last of his coffee and got to his feet, stretching lazily in a way that emphasised his already impressive height, his dark power seeming almost frightening in contrast to the restrained elegance of her father's decor.

'If you'll wait a sec I can kill two birds with one stone. I'll bring my case in from the car and you can show me which is my room.'

'I can *what*?'

Catherine could only stare at him in frank disbelief as he came to stand beside her, his closeness suddenly overwhelming.

It had to be the confined space of the doorframe together with her own already heightened vulnerability as a result of the way she was dressed, she told herself. It couldn't actually be the case that he grew bigger and stronger every time she looked at him. It was just her imagination working overtime.

But all the same she felt her nerves twist in sudden response, the tiny hairs on the back of her neck lifting in a devastating mixture of apprehension and sensual reaction that was as potent as a Molotov cocktail.

He was so near that she could see the yellow flecks in his eyes, gleaming like gold-dust on the bed of some deep river, and the tangy fragrance of his aftershave combined disturbingly with the clean, warm scent of his body, making her want to twitch her nose in the response of some small animal sniffing the air to track its mate.

'You can show me to my room.'

Evan's smile was easy, apparently relaxed, but she caught the glint of challenge deep in those sea-coloured eyes and knew that the subject was not up for discussion. It had been decided, signed and sealed, and her feelings on the matter were simply irrelevant.

'Your father and I talked it over last night after you'd gone to bed and decided that it would be better and easier if I came to stay here for a while.'

Better and easier for who? Catherine wondered, hastily suppressing the urge to turn a reproving glare on her father. He hadn't warned her about this, probably knowing that she wouldn't like the thought of Evan invading her privacy in this way. Privately she cursed the weakness that had driven her to retire to bed early.

She had pleaded tiredness as an excuse, in reality needing desperately to get away and seek the sanctuary of her bedroom, wanting peace and privacy in which to adjust to the turn of events that seemed to have swept her off her feet with the force of a tidal wave. She had also needed a reprieve from the overwhelming impact of Evan's powerful personality, feeling unable to stay in the same room as him a moment longer.

As a result, Evan and Lloyd had arranged things to suit them—or rather to suit Evan, it seemed.

But the decision had been made now, and she refused to let Evan see how much it troubled her.

'Fine. If you fetch your things, I'll take you up now,' she said, with what she hoped was a convincing airiness, stepping back to let him past.

She turned on her father as soon as the door had closed behind Evan. 'You might have warned me, Dad!'

'I knew you wouldn't like it.' Lloyd looked embarrassed but determined. 'But it seemed the best idea when Evan suggested it. After all, I leave for Japan on Monday, and you do need some sort of protection.'

'But do I have to share my home with him?'

'Evan thought you might find it a bit awkward.'

'Awkward!' Exasperation pitched Catherine's voice several octaves higher than usual. 'That has to be the

understatement of the year! Dad, I hardly know the man.
All I do know is that since six o'clock last night—' was
it really only fourteen hours ago? '—he seems to have
moved in on my life, taken it out of my hands, and is
now running it to suit his own preferences. He's a
stranger, Dad, an arrogant, objectionably bossy
stranger—and I'm supposed to share my home with
someone I don't know from Adam.'

'Which is precisely why I suggested that I move in
today,' Evan said quietly from behind her, making her
jump, her heart pounding in startled confusion. He must
have moved like greased lightning to get to his car and
back in that time, and she hadn't even heard him. For
such a big man he moved amazingly quietly, silent as a
hunting cat.

'Don't creep up on me like that!' She used annoyance
to cover the uncertainty of not knowing precisely what
he had overheard.

'I didn't creep,' Evan pointed out, with what Catherine
privately thought was excessive care. 'It's just that you
were so involved in your tirade that you wouldn't have
heard an army if it had come through the door. You
need to keep more alert. This man we're dealing with
isn't playing—you have to keep your wits about you at
all times.'

The reproof in his tone was mild but it was there, and
deep down Catherine knew she deserved it. She had been
so caught up in her own personal feelings that she had
forgotten the real reason why Evan was here.

The memory of the horror that had swept over her
on the previous night at the realisation that Joe had once
more tracked her down was a sobering reminder of just
how much worse she would have felt if Evan hadn't been
there to intercept the phone call. Suddenly that phrase,
'This man *we're* dealing with,' sounded infinitely
comforting.

'Yes, you're right.'

Her smile was rueful, touched with contrition. If this was going to work, she had to be less prickly—at least give it a try. After all, Evan was here to *help* her. She should remember that.

'Well, we'd better get you settled in. Which bedroom had you allocated to Evan, Dad?'

'Any...' Her father was checking through the contents of his briefcase. 'Mrs B said that all the spare rooms are aired and left ready, with the beds made up, so you can choose.'

He snapped the case shut with a brusque movement and shot a concerned look at the clock.

'Look, I really should be going—'

'Of course—you get off.' Catherine could only stare as once more Evan took charge, for all the world as if this was *his* home and not her father's. 'Catherine and I have plenty to do—and it's time we got better acquainted.'

'I know she'll be safe with you.'

Lloyd seemed blithely oblivious to the fact that his daughter didn't share his easy confidence. The safety she didn't doubt—at least not where defence against Joe was concerned. It was her own mental balance that was in danger of being severely shaken.

'Bye sweetheart.' Her father dropped his customary peck on her cheek. 'Have a good day. Take care of her, Evan.'

'Have a good day'. It really rather depended on how you defined the term 'good', Catherine thought, watching with a sense of disbelief as Evan, who had followed the older man into the hall, firmly closed and then locked the door behind him.

On one level she acknowledged the necessity for such an action, appreciating Evan's thoroughness in checking on her security, but on another she couldn't stop herself from resenting the way his actions seemed to drive home the message that he had well and truly taken over control and she was just a bit player in her own life, standing on the sidelines like an afterthought.

She had better start asserting her rights, and quickly, because if she wasn't careful Evan would become every bit as much of an invader as Joe, and she wouldn't be able to decide which one of them was having the most disturbing effect on her peace of mind.

CHAPTER FOUR

'MAY I remind you that this is my father's house—my home?'

'Oh, I'm sorry.' Evan turned wide, innocent eyes on Catherine's indignant face, his smile brilliant, totally disconcerting her. 'Did you want to lock the door yourself? I didn't realise it mattered so much.'

'No— I mean—of course it doesn't!'

Put like that, how could she say anything else? To protest any further would only have made herself sound foolish and petulant.

'It's just that I wish you'd remember...'

The sudden change in his face dried the words on her tongue. As swiftly as it had come that innocent look vanished, to be replaced by a new hardness.

'Remember what?' His voice was ominously quiet now. 'That I'm just the hired help and should know my place?'

So he had caught her comment to Ellie last night, and it had rankled. But then, of course, she hadn't known his real position.

'Well, not in the way you mean—but I do think that this isn't going to work unless we lay down a few ground rules.'

'Is that so?' If the mock innocence of a few moments before had disconcerted her, then the amusement that now lurked in those blue-green eyes now threatened her already shaky sense of self-control. 'Tell me, are you always this grouchy in the mornings?'

'No, I'm not!' Catherine returned indignantly. 'As a matter of fact, I'm usually very much a morning sort of

53

person. I like to get up with the birds, and I'm not one of those people who needs several cups of coffee before I can get going. Generally—'

'So this isn't general?'

'No.' She wished she'd said normally, because this certainly wasn't normal!

'So it's personal.' It was a statement not a question.

'Personal'. Something about that word made Catherine shiver faintly. The thought of getting personal with Evan sent a feeling like the crackle of static sliding across her skin, sensitising every nerve so that even her bare toes curled into the thickness of the carpet beneath her feet.

'Not at all!' she declared sharply. 'Please don't make this into something it isn't, Mr Lindsay. Now, if you'll follow me—' it was very difficult to be dignified and aloof when wearing a baby-doll nightdress '—I'll show you to your room. Is that all you have?'

Evan followed the line of her gaze to the grey canvas holdall that lay at his feet.

'I believe in travelling light,' he returned laconically. 'There is no point in weighing yourself down with a lot of unnecessary clutter, especially when a job's only temporary.'

'I'm impressed! I have to admit that even on a week's holiday I'm one of those people who has to pack everything but the kitchen sink—and even then I worry that there's something I've forgotten.'

'Then we obviously have very different priorities in life.'

'We'll have to agree to differ. You clearly don't plan on staying long.'

'Trying to get rid of me already?'

She was turning towards the stairs as Evan spoke, and she was grateful for the fact that her back was to him and he couldn't see her wince at the sting of his irony.

'Not at all, Mr Lindsay.' She refused to let him see that his words had had any effect. 'I was just wondering how long you thought it would take to persuade this Joe that he's on to a loser and make him give up—'

Suddenly she stopped dead and turned to the man behind her, unable to hide her true feelings.

'You do think he *will* give up, don't you?'

'Eventually.'

Those changeable eyes were suddenly dark as moss, looking deep into her face, and the low voice was soft and slightly husky.

'But I promise you one thing...' His gaze held hers with the effortless control of a mesmerist. 'I'll be here with you right to the bitter end, however long it takes.'

It was as it had been on the previous night, Catherine thought dazedly. That same inexplicable rush of irrational trust and belief in him, only more so. This time it was mixed with something new—a disturbing sensuality that pulsed warmly through her as if heated by the glow in his eyes, an intense awareness of the soft sound of his breathing, the way his dark hair gleamed in a shaft of light from the window.

'Thank you.'

It was just a whisper, drawn from her almost unconsciously, and for a few more long, silent seconds that mesmerist's gaze held her transfixed, oblivious to anything but him. But then, abruptly, as if coming back to himself from a long distance away, Evan shook himself slightly.

'And I thought we agreed on Evan.' The matter of factness of his tone was like a dash of cold water in her face, making her blink hard.

'So we did.'

The trance that had held her was shattered, and, released from its hold, Catherine almost ran up the rest of the flight of stairs, only realising as she reached the landing that she had been holding her breath so fiercely that now she had to let it go in a heavy, gasping sigh.

'Your room is here.'

She spoke rapidly to cover the shaken force of her reaction, the pounding of her heart so loud in her own ears that she was sure he must hear it too as she moved swiftly along the landing, ignoring the first four doors and finally pushing open the one right at the far end.

'I think you'll have everything you need, but if you don't, just ask. I'll send Mrs Bentley up with some towels when—'

She broke off uncertainly as she saw the frown with which Evan surveyed the blue and white decor of the room. It was a frown she couldn't comprehend. There was nothing wrong with the bedroom that she could see.

'Which is your bedroom?' The question was sharp to the point of curtness.

'Just along here, but—'

'Show me!'

'Mr Lindsay—'

'Evan,' he corrected harshly. 'I want to see which is your room.'

Suddenly she realised what he wanted.

'Of course—you want to check it out from a security point of view—to case the joint.'

The attempt at a joke fell painfully flat as Evan simply ignored it, pushing open the door she had indicated with such force that it slammed back against the wall. Standing in the doorway, he surveyed the rose and cream decor with a narrow-eyed scrutiny that made Catherine feel as if each of her belongings was some sort of specimen under a microscope, awaiting dissection by his probing gaze.

With his laconic, 'I believe in travelling light,' in her mind, she suddenly saw the array of books and magazines, the cosmetics on the dressing-table, the shelves of miniature china cats left over from her adolescence, even the battered teddy bear on the bed as a collection of trivia—the reflection of a cluttered mind.

'For someone who didn't even dare to go back to her flat to collect any clothes, you seem to have made yourself very comfortable.'

Uneasy at the way he had made her feel about her room, and by implication herself, she rounded on him sharply.

'Are you implying that I wasn't really as scared as I made out? That I took time to worry about cosmetics and things—that my appearance mattered more to me than my safety? Or perhaps you actually think that I exaggerated my fear in order to—to—' She faltered as once more the full force of that aquamarine gaze was turned on her.

'To do what? Ensure the pleasure of my company?' His tone mocked her. 'Did I say that?'

'You implied—'

'I implied nothing. I merely commented that for a temporary hide-out this room looks remarkably well lived-in.'

'Most of the stuff was mine when I lived at home. Dad said I could leave it so that I could always have a base here—but I suppose you're going to say that, like my car, it's a dead giveaway to anyone checking out the place.'

'You're learning.' Evan's response was dry. 'It also reveals a lot about your character.'

Once more that sea-coloured gaze swept round the room, twisting something deep inside Catherine as she was forced to wonder what that cool, analytical brain was thinking. She had a sudden, almost uncontrollable urge to pick up the elderly teddy bear and hold it against herself as a defence against his probing eyes, feeling disturbingly vulnerable as if she had suddenly been stripped completely naked before him.

'And little of it complimentary, to judge from your tone.' Inner tension made her voice tight and hostile.

The look Evan turned on her matched the wide-eyed innocence he had assumed earlier.

'You really are snippy, aren't you?' he drawled tauntingly. 'Who pulled your chain?'

It was time to stop pretending, Catherine decided, glaring up at him, her blue eyes brilliant with annoyance.

'I can't help it—you know how it is sometimes.'

Evan looked blank and uncomprehending—deliberately so, she was convinced.

'No, I can't say I do—but I'm sure you're going to tell me.'

'I can't explain it.' Catherine gritted her teeth against the fury that threatened to spit fire at his goading. 'But sometimes it's just an instinct thing—some people get your back up.'

'And I do that to you?'

'Yes, you do!'

If she hadn't known better, Catherine might have been tempted to believe in his carefully calculated expression of hurt. As it was, even distrusting it as she did, she found that some weak, vulnerable part of her mind was responding to it on a very primitive, instinctive level, and an over-sensitive conscience reproved her for being unnecessarily harsh.

Unnecessarily and dishonestly so, strict honesty told her. It was true that Evan's presence put her on edge, but not quite in the way that she had said.

With him standing there so big and strong, his dark colouring and clothes in such stark contrast to the feminine prettiness of the room, she couldn't help but be aware of him in a way that threatened her composure, her sense of inner security. He was so forcefully, elementally, intensely *male*, in a way that seemed to call to every female cell in her body, bringing it to tingling life in a new and very disturbing way.

She was almost fearfully sensitive to the contrast between her own slender height and his potent power, and although that face, with its broken nose, could never be described as strictly handsome, it had a rugged attractiveness that had far more impact than any more conventional good looks.

'I'm—sorry...' An uneasy conscience made her lessen the force of her declaration, even if she couldn't bring herself to admit the reality of her mixed-up emotions.

'You can't help how you feel.' Evan's response was indifferent, but then he turned to her, looking deep into her eyes once more. 'But one thing, Catherine—this isn't going to work unless we're together on it. I can't help you unless you want to be helped. It has to be a joint enterprise—we need to be partners.'

It was happening again, that strange, almost hypnotic feeling, the sense of being drawn out of herself and losing all control. This time she found herself concentrating on the mouth that spoke those words, beautifully shaped, designed to give pleasure, the sharply defined upper lip set off by the fuller, more sensual lower one. She couldn't stop herself from wondering what it would be like to have those lips kiss her...

'Catherine?'

The sharpening of Evan's tone penetrated the smoky haze that clouded her thoughts, snapping her back to reality with such a jolt that she closed her eyes swiftly, fearful that he might read the wanton direction of her thoughts in them.

'You do understand?'

'Yes,' she said on a sigh. 'I understand.'

She opened her eyes to an empty space. Evan had gone and was moving purposefully down the landing, collecting his holdall from the bedroom she had allocated and then before she had quite realised what he had in mind, flinging open the door of the one adjoining hers without so much as a by your leave.

'What—?' she began, though she didn't really need to ask. Her suspicions were confirmed by the way that Evan slung his bag up onto the bed, unzipping it firmly.

'*This* will be my room,' he declared, his tone of voice, the hard set of his face challenging her to object.

'But you can't—I mean—the other—'

'The other bedroom is too far away from yours. If I'm in here I'll be able to hear every sound you make.'

Which was precisely what worried her. The thought of his being in here at night, listening to the faint sounds of her undressing, showering in the *en suite* bathroom, getting into bed, made the tiny hairs on her skin lift in a shivery response. It was all too personal, too intrusive, too *invasive*; too thoroughly unsettling ever to contemplate.

And when her mind threw at her the fact that lying in the darkness in her own room she would be able to do exactly the same as she had just imagined him doing, she felt a rush of panic that knocked her way off balance mentally.

'No! You can't— I won't—!'

With some vague, half-formed idea of snatching his bag, returning it—and, hopefully, him—to the room she had originally selected, she lurched forward, her hand outstretched. But in her rush she didn't notice that the tie-belt on her robe had worked loose and was trailing on the floor. She caught her foot in it, stumbling heavily with the white sash tangling like a snake around her ankles.

'Evan!' It was a cry of shock as she went flying, throwing out a despairing hand to stop herself, knowing it was already too late.

'Hey!'

She never hit the ground. In one swift movement Evan was at her side, his hands coming out to support her, fastening firmly around her waist. The next moment he swung her up off her feet with an ease that revealed the true strength of the muscles outlined by the clinging T-shirt, and she was held tightly, close against the warm strength of his body.

'Evan . . .' Catherine said again, but on a new and very different note this time, because her heart was racing, jolting into a fluttering, uneven rhythm that made it impossible to speak naturally, the words coming out in a breathless rush.

'It's all right, I've got you,' Evan said softly, and although she knew that the words were supposed to reassure, in fact they had precisely the opposite effect.

It wasn't just shock or even a sense of relief that was making her head spin, instead it was another very different reaction, one that was purely in response to the effect that Evan's nearness was having on every one of her senses—not that there was anything pure about it!

She was supremely and very physically aware of the warmth of his body reaching her through the thin material of her robe, the powerful expanse of his chest under her cheek, the iron grip that held her. She was held so close to him that she could catch the faint tangy scent of the swimming pool still lingering on his skin and hair, and underneath it was the warm, musky essence of his body, much more potent than any artificially created perfume.

But what about Evan himself? Did he feel this too—this quivering, electrical response, the tingling awakening of every nerve-end, the sensation like the slow, tentative uncurling of some new and very delicate plant deep inside? Needing to know, she tilted her head back against his shoulder in order to look up into his face, and a convulsive shudder of reaction ran through her as she saw the darkness of his eyes, the way they seemed as immeasurably deep as any distant ocean.

'Cat . . .' he murmured, and her name was like a sigh, a warm breath feathering across her skin, making her shiver in the steel-hard grip of his arms.

'Evan...'

She had never known such an instant response, never felt the blood burn in her veins in this way, betraying colour rushing to her cheeks while her use of his name was a shaken expression of the need that she couldn't put into words, a need she could scarcely define, even to herself, until he interpreted what she was trying to say with devastating accuracy, his dark head lowering as his lips captured hers.

She had known this feeling once before, Catherine thought hazily as that sensual mouth took possession of hers with a force that made her mind reel. A long time ago, as an inexperienced swimmer, she had ventured out too far into a sea that had suddenly changed from being as calm and placid as a sunlit pool to a turbulent mixture of deceptive currents and wild, crashing waves. Caught by a dangerous undertow, she had been pulled down, down, down, the water breaking over her head, blinding her, driving all thought from her mind.

She hadn't been able to see, nor hear, had only been able to feel, floating without direction, buffeted backwards and forwards at the whim of the wild element that had enclosed her, and knowing only one thing—that she was well and truly out of her depth and had no idea how or even if she was going to survive this devastating experience.

And then, at last, after what had seemed like an age, not knowing whether minutes or only seconds had passed, she had surfaced again, her head coming above the water as she gasped frantically, painfully dragging in much needed air just as she did now, when Evan's mouth ceased its tormentingly sensual exploration of her own and his head finally lifted.

'Evan—' She tried to find the words to communicate her feelings but none would come.

And he had only moved in order to make his position more comfortable. She found that she was being carried across the room, that Evan was laying her down on the bed, pausing only to sweep aside his bag with scant regard for the way it landed unceremoniously on the floor before he came down beside her, his long legs stretched out on the navy cotton duvet cover.

His arms came round her again, warm and strong, and as her blood once more ran hotly in her veins it was as if all the tension in her body had melted away in its warmth, every limb, every muscle—almost, it seemed, every bone—becoming pliant and soft against his hardness.

'Is this what you want, Cat?' The question was a soft murmur against her cheek, the words feathering over her skin like the most delicate caress.

'Mmm . . .'

She was incapable of words, intent only on the pleasure his hands were giving her as the strong fingers began to trace soft, erotic patterns down the side of her face, along her neck. Only now, when it had eased, did she realise just how painfully that tension had gripped her, stretching every muscle tight until it ached, so that now the release from it was almost as intoxicating as some potently alcoholic drink.

'And this?'

She didn't notice that her robe had gone until she felt Evan's hands, warm and strong, on the soft flesh of her throat and shoulders, smoothly stroking, moving down, down, so close to where the tops of her breasts were exposed by the low, scooped neckline that she writhed in delight, a shaft of desire, sharp as a knife, stabbing through her as the unthinking movement brought her hard up against the strength of his body, her pale, slim legs tangling with his long, muscular ones, the harshness of the denim rough against her skin.

Moments later that ache of desire spread through the rest of her body as the path his hands had followed was trailed by the caress of his mouth, the tiny, shoestring

straps of her nightdress swiftly brushed aside to allow
him access to the sensitive breasts that seemed to strain
against the delicate fabric, mutely inviting his possession. The firm, slightly abrasive touch of his hard
palms as he cupped the soft, warm weight made her gasp
aloud in amazement and delight at the speed with which
gentle pleasure could turn to a fierce, demanding need
deep inside.

'Is this how you want it to be?'

Evan's voice was rougher, harsh with an echo of her
own passionate response, and she shivered with excitement as his fingers, harder now and more demanding, slid slowly upwards, digging into her shoulders
for a second before moving to encircle her neck.

'Or is *this* what you want?'

Catherine's heart gave a violent jolt of shock, almost
seeming to stop dead as the hands that until now had
been so gently caressing, teasingly arousing, creating
patterns of delight in pleasure spots she hadn't known
she possessed, suddenly clenched harshly, closing hard
around her throat, tightening...

'Evan!' Her voice was just a croak of protest. 'Stop
it! You're frightening me!'

To her horror, he didn't react in the way she had anticipated, making no move to release her and not looking
in the least contrite. Instead he lifted his head to stare
deep into her eyes, his expression coldly unyielding, his
eyes as icy as the frozen seas of the Arctic—emotionless,
dead.

All trace of the desire that had warmed her fled from
Catherine's body, leaving her desolate and shiveringly
afraid, her lips parting on a cry of panicked distress as
the pressure at her throat intensified, cruel fingers digging
painfully into soft flesh in a way that she knew would
already have marked and bruised.

'*Evan*!—you're *frightening* me!'

'Am I?'

The trace of dark laughter in his tone was even more terrifying than anything that had gone before, and Catherine's mind whirled with such a sense of terrified desperation that the buzzing inside her head was like the sound of a thousand trapped and angry bees. She was afraid she might lose consciousness, might actually pass out, leaving herself completely at his mercy.

'Am I frightening you, Cat? I hope so—or do you like flirting with danger? Is that what turns you on?'

And then, with a suddenness that was as devastating in its abruptness as his shocking assault on her, he released her, his hands dropping from her neck as he levered his long body up and away from her so that he stood, towering over her threateningly as she cowered against the pillows, her eyes pansy-dark pools of shock above colourless cheeks.

'Did I really scare you, Cat?' he asked, with a softness that was infinitely disturbing when contrasted with the controlled savagery of moments before.

'You terrified me!' Catherine flung at him, watching him warily all the time, ready to react swiftly if he made any sort of movement. The dangerous mood that had gripped him seemed to be ebbing away, but all the same she didn't dare take any risks or assume that she was safe. Quite frankly, she didn't trust him one tiny bit.

'Good.'

The dark satisfaction in his voice was hateful to her ears, making her want to lash out at him, but even as she controlled the impulsive movement, telling herself that discretion was the better part of valour, he suddenly smiled in a way that had her reeling back against the pillows once more.

'Now perhaps you'll learn.'

'Learn?' Catherine could scarcely believe what she was hearing.

Evan nodded curtly, aquamarine eyes burning into her wide, shocked blue ones.

'You need to learn that in a situation like this you can't trust anyone. This guy—this bloody Joe—could be anyone at all—someone you know.'

He paused—deliberately, Catherine knew—to give an added emphasis to what came next.

'He could even be me.'

CHAPTER FIVE

'CATHERINE! Cat—are you still in there?'

'Go away!' Catherine growled, heedless of the fact that her words were drowned by the noise of the shower's rushing water.

'Cat?'

Swearing under her breath, Catherine reached up and turned off the shower with an abrupt movement, slanting a furious glare in the direction of the securely locked bathroom door.

'*Go away!*' she yelled into the sudden silence.

'That's what I'm trying to tell you.' Evan's voice from the other side of the door was surprisingly good-tempered. 'I have to go out.'

'For good, I hope,' Catherine muttered to herself.

'What? Did you say something? Catherine, this isn't exactly the easiest way to conduct a conversation. Why don't you—?'

'Open the door so that we can communicate more easily?' Catherine derided. 'And give you another opportunity to grope me? Not damn likely—what sort of a fool do you think I am?'

The last words came out on a disturbing quaver as a sudden, embarrassing awareness of her naked state gripped her. Even with the thickness of the door between herself and Evan she felt uneasily vulnerable, a cold, creeping sensation moving over her skin in a way that had nothing to do with the natural cooling down that followed her turning off the hot water.

Hastily she stepped out of the shower cubicle and reached for a huge peach-coloured towel, wrapping it firmly round her.

'I never took you for a fool, Cat—just rather fool-hardy, far too trusting for your own good. But at least you've just proved you're learning—'

'You're damn right I am!'

Catherine pulled the towel more tightly round her, re-fusing to let herself acknowledge the way that every inch of her body still seemed to be in a state of heightened awareness, so that the brush of the fluffy cotton across it was an exquisite form of sensual torture. If she had hoped that the heat and force of the water, the deter-mination with which she had scrubbed at herself would have erased the feel of Evan's touch and subdued her mutinous senses into submission, then she had been severely mistaken.

'So now you've proved your point why don't you just leave me alone?'

'That was exactly what I had in mind, but I thought I'd better warn you—'

'What?'

The shock that ripped through her had her dashing to the door and wrenching it open, heedless of her un-dressed state.

'You're leaving! But you can't! I mean—'

Moments before she might have wished for just this, in fact, standing under the hot shower, she had wished him anywhere but here—in hell, preferably, or some-where equally uncomfortable. Her skin had flamed at the thought of the way she had let him kiss and caress her, anger flaring at the way he could talk so hypocriti-cally about trust when in fact he had abused her trust in such a way.

If she could have, she would have sacked him at once, but her father had to go to Japan, and she knew he would never agree to leave her alone. *She* didn't want to be left to face Joe on her own.

'You can't just abandon me...'

Her voice failed, the words drying in her throat as she saw those sea-coloured eyes slide away from her flushed face, unbecomingly framed by soaking hair that the water had turned from her natural ash-blonde into an unflattering dark mouse.

Just for a split second he let his gaze linger on the soft roundness of her shoulders above the peach towel, the touch of his eyes almost a physical thing, bringing a hot rush of colour to her skin—colour that deepened to a fiery red as his gaze flicked back up to meet hers. But she saw no sign of any sensual appreciation, or even interest in it, just a coldly scathing contempt that stung as sharply as if he had struck her painfully with a riding whip.

'You're doing it again, Catherine.' For all the softness of his tone, it had the bitter bite of acid, and she flinched away from his hard-faced scorn. 'You really must think before you act.'

'I—but—'

A fierce inner struggle with her own feelings made it impossible to get the words out in any coherent form. In the moment that those cold blue-green eyes had swept back up to her face she had been a prey to such a disconcertingly unexpected rush of feeling that she could hardly believe it herself.

Could she really have felt *disappointed* by the lack of interest he had showed? Was she really such a weak fool that one humiliation at his hands wasn't enough for her? Was she actually prepared to subject herself to another?

'I—' she started again, then jumped fearfully as Evan moved suddenly towards her. Acting purely instinctively, she shrank back against the door, her hands coming up defensively, ready to fight if necessary.

But he simply ignored her response, reaching past her to snatch up the green and navy striped towelling bathrobe that hung on a hook in the still steamy bathroom, and flinging it in her direction, careless of whether she was ready to catch it or not.

'Put that on,' he ordered, the harshness of his tone combining with her confusion about his motives to make her hands shake nervously as she fumbled with the thick towelling, trying to push her arms into the sleeves without letting go of the towel she still had wrapped around her.

As the robe was actually her father's, and therefore more than a couple of sizes too large, she was able to get it on over the towel, pulling it close and belting it firmly, heedless of the way that the extra padding made her look like a sack of lumpy potatoes with a piece of string tied round the middle.

'Very flattering,' Evan commented drily, the gleam in his eye and the lazy irony of his tone adding fuel to the blaze of indignation inside her head.

But perhaps it was better this way, she told herself ruefully, after all, she didn't want him to find her in any way attractive. The memory of the scene in the bedroom, the knowledge that she had been playing with a very dangerous fire indeed, and had only just escaped being extremely badly burned, made her feel alternately burning hot and then shiveringly cold just to think of it. She certainly didn't want to risk a repetition, no matter how much her disloyal body might seem to have the memory of the pleasure it had felt imprinted into its skin like some long-ago brand.

'I thought that was what you wanted!' she flashed at him. 'I thought you expected me to look like some old bag lady without an ounce of sex appeal!'

'Hardly that,' he put in mildly, but, launched on her tirade, pushed over the edge of control by the conflicting feelings warring inside her, she ignored his interjection, rushing on thoughtlessly.

'So that no man in his right mind would be in the least bit interested in me. That way this Joe, whoever he is, will be so turned off simply by the sight of me that he'll turn his attentions elsewhere and I'll be left in peace—'

The last word was choked off, because it was only as she said the words that she realised just how much she hoped for that sort of peace. Enough to put up with Evan's autocratic behaviour? Her mind threw the question at her, and with a sense of despair she knew that there could only be one answer.

'I doubt that I could manage that.'

Evan's voice was the low, softly enticing one he had used to such effect earlier, and, remembering what that had led to, Catherine instinctively stiffened her resolve against him.

'For one thing, nothing on God's earth could make you look like a bag lady. Even with your hair hanging down in rat's tails like that, and not a scrap of make-up on—'

Abruptly he caught himself up, breaking off what he had been about to say and raking one strong hand through the darkness of his hair, taking a deep, uneven breath before he spoke again.

'You'll always be a classy lady.' If he had meant it to be a compliment it didn't sound that way, his dismissive tone throwing the comment away as of no importance. 'But if we're talking about Joe, then, yes, my aim is to make sure that he does leave you alone—for good. And I'll do everything in my power to make sure that happens.'

'But—you said—' Catherine frowned her confusion. 'I thought you were leaving.'

Evan shook his head firmly, a touch of dry humour gleaming in the deep sea pools of his eyes.

'I said I was going out. *You* assumed I was leaving. Wish-fulfilment, perhaps? All I'm doing is taking your car and putting it somewhere safe. I'll be back as quickly as I can.'

'You *are* coming back, then?'

She didn't know whether she was relieved or disappointed. She seemed to be fated to be subjected to conflicting, ambiguous feelings where this man was concerned.

'Oh, yes...'

She would have sworn that it was impossible for his voice to drop any lower, become any more gentle, but somehow he managed it, the soft tones whispering over her skin in a way that made her shiver in uncontrollable reaction.

'I'll be back. You don't get rid of me that easily. You see, there's one thing you should know about me, Cat, and that is that I never leave a job half done. When I commit myself to something, I always see it through— right to the bitter end.'

'And you're—committed—to me?'

If she had had ambiguous feelings earlier, they were as nothing to the emotions that seemed to knot in her throat at the thought of that.

'To keeping you safe,' Evan corrected coolly. 'And in order to do so I'd better get your car away from here. Don't worry— I'll treat it as if it were my own,' he added cynically, misinterpreting the sudden flare of concern in her eyes. 'I'm a very experienced driver.'

'I'm sure you are!' Catherine returned sharply, unsettled by the stab of pique she had felt in response to his subtle change of emphasis earlier. 'In fact, I'm sure you're "experienced" in most things.'

One dark eyebrow lifted in quizzical response to her muttered undertone.

'Is that a challenge, Cat? Perhaps one day I'll take you up on it—but right now I have more important things to deal with. You never did give me the car keys.'

And they both knew precisely why she hadn't done so, Catherine thought, a sour taste rising in her mouth as she flounced past him, nose in the air, into her bedroom to collect the keys. The haughty movement she had aimed for was rather spoiled by the cumbersome bulk of the combined layers of towelling, which made walking awkward and clumsy, but she kept her head held high and waddled as swiftly as possible to where her handbag lay on the bed.

'Here—'

She tossed the keys towards him, a touch of spite that she couldn't quite suppress making her aim them so that they fell short of his outstretched hand, forcing him to take a couple of steps forward into the room and bend down in order to pick them up.

'Thanks.'

His tone was deliberately edged with a note that made her shiver in spite of the bulky padding, one that was at odds with the casual indifference of Evan's actions as he tossed the bunch of keys from one hand to another.

'Now, will you be OK while I'm out? I promise I'll be away as little time as possible—an hour at the very most—but it'd be best to take no chances.'

His voice had changed again, Catherine recognised. Gone was the soft, enticing quality that had seduced her earlier, and in its place was a cold, hard forcefulness, the effect of which was like being hit in the face by a bucket of iced water. This steely-eyed character was a very different kettle of fish from the man who had inspired her with such confidence, with such a feeling of trust only a short time before.

This man made all the nerves in her stomach twist into tight, painful knots, her heart seeming to leap up, to start beating high in her throat when he moved unexpectedly. Seeing him like this, so imposingly tall and strong, his features set into that inimical expression, she could only be grateful that he was on her side.

Or was he? The sudden, stabbing question was like a shaft of light illuminating a darkened room, making her remember how it had felt to have that ruthless determination, that single-minded force turned on her for other than selfless reasons.

Evan had manipulated her coldly and unemotionally, reducing her to a helpless wreck, playing on feelings, responses she hadn't known she possessed, pressing buttons she hadn't even been aware of, purely for his own cruel ends. And she had been putty in his hands—weak, foolish and so easily swayed, she berated herself furiously.

'So when I leave, you make sure the door is firmly locked behind me,' Evan continued, oblivious to the desire to lock that door behind him once and for all that had now taken root inside Catherine's head. 'And don't answer the phone or ring anyone—*anyone* at all. If someone calls and it's important they'll ring back when I'm here to screen all calls.

'Is that understood, Catherine?' he added when, still absorbed in the delightful vision of locking him out, she didn't respond. 'Have you got that clear?'

'Perfectly.'

'And *get dressed*!'

'Yes, sir!'

Sketching a satirical salute in response to his emphatic tone, she suddenly rebelled, turning defiant blue eyes on his hard-boned face.

'But if you've finished issuing orders, I think it's about time I had my turn—time we established those ground rules I mentioned.'

'Such as?'

The laconic question was threaded through with something dark and ominous, and this time the lift to one eyebrow had nothing of the touch of humour that had lightened it before.

'Well—' she forced herself not to be put off by his attitude '—for a start, this is the last time you come into my room without my permission. I suppose I can't stop you from sleeping next door, but from now on you do not come in here without my express say-so.' And hell could freeze over before she'd give that! 'Is that clear?' Deliberately she echoed his own curtness.

'Crystal.'

'And you can keep your hands—and anything else— strictly to yourself. You're here to protect me, not maul me around...' Her confidence faded under the force of the dark scowl that crossed his face. 'Is—that understood?'

'Perfectly.' The salute he sketched and his tone made a mockery of her indignation, echoing as they did her own gestures of just minutes before. 'Is there anything else?'

In spite of herself, Catherine had to fight to suppress the smile that threatened, tugging up the corners of her mouth in response to the wicked, teasing glance he slanted her. With an effort she forced them down again.

'That'll do for now. If I think of anything else, I'll let you know.'

'Oh, I'm sure you will. But in the meantime I'd better go and deal with that car. Remember to lock the door after me.'

'Yes, sir!'

'And for God's sake, *get dressed*!'

The last words floated up the stairwell as he ran down to the hall, taking two steps at once all the way. He paused in the doorway, looking back up at her.

'Oh—and Catherine...'

'Yes?'

'I never *maul*.'

Then he was gone, and a moment later the sound of the front door slamming echoed through the house. The silence that followed it was suddenly intense, and very disturbing. Catherine had never felt quite so alone, so terribly vulnerable. Evan had barely left the house, and already she felt lost without him.

For a long, taut moment, she stood frozen to the spot, staring blankly at the door through which he had left, but then the sound of a car's engine outside—*her* car's engine, she thought bitterly—pushed her into action, and she followed Evan's path down the stairs, ramming the key into the door and turning it with a force that expressed her disturbed feelings.

'"Lock the door after me",' she muttered, drawing satisfaction from the fact that, for a while at least, Evan Lindsay couldn't get back into the house unless she chose to let him. '"And get dressed",' she added satirically, bounding back upstairs with a new sense of freedom at the thought of having the place to herself.

Her mood sobered again abruptly as she surveyed the scant array of clothing in her wardrobe, reminding her of the rush with which she had fled from her flat, taking nothing with her—these few items being all she had left at her father's house.

'Wear something comfortable and practical.' Evan's voice sounded inside her head. 'Jeans and a T-shirt...'

If only he knew, she thought resignedly, pulling a lavender T-shirt and a clean but worn pair of denim jeans from their hangers. Much as she might have liked to rebel against his dictatorial commands, she couldn't. She had nothing else to choose from.

A sudden rush of very feminine pride made her wish that her wardrobe was more extensive. If only she had had a chance to pick up one or two of the items that were in her cupboards back at her flat. She would have loved to see Evan's face if she'd appeared in one of *them*. Once, just once, she would have liked to knock him dead.

Almost as soon as she had thought the words she drew herself up short, staring at her reflection in the mirror with eyes that were dark blue with shock.

What *was* she thinking of? Evan Lindsay had already proved himself to be the sort of man possessed of the sort of cold-blooded ruthlessness that had shown itself in the nasty scene in his bedroom only an hour or so before. He had used her body and her feelings callously and calculatedly in order to make a point—and this was the man she was thinking of trying to *attract*!

She needed her head examining! Really, when it came down to it, it was a toss-up as to which was worse—him or Joe...

That thought reminded her on a shiver of apprehension that she still hadn't got dressed and was wandering round the house looking unflatteringly like some oversized Michelin man, still padded up in the double layer of towelling. She would feel decidedly better when she had some proper clothing on.

She did. Once in the T-shirt and jeans, with a touch of tinted moisturiser, to give her cheeks a look of having been warmed by the sun, and some brown mascara on her long lashes, she felt much more capable of coping with anything the day might throw at her, even humming softly to herself as she dried her hair, brushing it into a sleek, pale bell around her face.

As if to test her resolve, it was just at that point that the telephone rang in the hall below, freezing the brush in mid-stroke.

'Don't answer the phone,' Evan had commanded, and, quite honestly, the thought of just lifting the receiver made her heart race uncomfortably.

But what if it was Ellie, ringing back to find out just why she had been so unceremoniously cut off the night before? Or it could be her father phoning from work. If she didn't answer he would be afraid that something was wrong. He would panic. But as the phone went on and on, its shrill sound echoing through the silent house, she knew she had to answer or go mad listening to it.

Her hand shook as she picked up the receiver, and instinctively the fingers of one hand crossed in a superstitious gesture against ill luck.

It didn't work.

'Hello, Honey.'

Just two words. Two words in that hateful, whispering voice, slightly distorted, as if he held a handkerchief or something similar over the mouthpiece to disguise it. But those two words meant that last night had not been a fluke, that she hadn't dreamed it. He knew where she was, and his sinsterly drawled greeting echoed over and over in her head. 'Hello, Honey.' 'Hello, Honey.' 'Hello, Honey.'

'Oh, go to hell!'

With a strength born of desperation, she dragged herself out of the trance into which the sound of his voice had sent her, slamming the receiver down onto its rest and then whirling round to where the phone was plugged in at the wall, yanking the wire out of its socket.

There, let him get at her now!

But then reaction set in. Her legs weakened beneath her, trembling in shock, so that eventually she sank down on the bottom step, curling her arms around her knees and hugging them tight, forming a curved, protective ball.

She didn't know how long she sat there; only knew that she found it impossible to move. She could only sit and stare at the telephone, her blue eyes wide and unfocused, as some fearful small animal might watch a predatory snake, waiting for it to strike.

Gradually the trembling panic eased; the nauseating churning in the pit of her stomach slowing until at last she felt able to move, but only into the safety of the living-room, its curtains still drawn concealingly against the brightness of the day.

Would she ever feel the same again? Was this how it felt to be a rabbit, hiding in its burrow, always fearful, unable to move, knowing that outside the hunter waited, eternally vigilant, demonically patient? What made it so much worse was not knowing who he was. If she could only put a real name—a face—to the evil that preyed on her, instead of just some nameless, faceless horror.

'No!'

Determinedly she straightened her spine. Letting him get to her like this was to let him win. Evan had been right about that. She had to make some sort of a move, even if it was only to get herself a cup of coffee, she told herself, heading for the kitchen.

But the silence of the house preyed on her nerves. She found herself jumping at every tiny sound, turning sharply to catch sight of something that she thought she had glimpsed out of the corner of her eye, only to find that it was just a figment of her imagination.

She had never known how it felt to be so completely, totally alone, and when the sound of footsteps on the gravel came to her from outside, she was too uptight to know whether the feeling that set her heart racing was relief or a worsening of the fear that had gripped her all morning.

She couldn't even nerve herself to peep out through the curtains, and she jumped like a frightened cat when the doorbell rang and someone rattled the handle, twisting it from outside.

'Hello!'

For a second she didn't recognise the voice, then realisation dawned, and she dashed to unlock the door, her hands shaking with relief.

'Evan!'

In the moment that she saw his tall, strong form in the doorway, all she could think was that she had never been so glad to see anyone in her life, and it was all that she could do to stop herself from reaching out, taking hold of his arms and dragging him into the house in her eagerness to have his forceful, protective presence close to her once more.

'Well, at least you've shown that you can follow instructions sometimes,' Evan remarked drily as he pulled the door firmly closed behind him. 'But I think it would be much better if I had a key to the house from now on. Have you got a spare or—? *Cat?* What is it?'

Those sharp aquamarine eyes had caught her pallor, the tension that gripped her slender body.

'What's happened?'

But then he caught sight of the unplugged phone, its cord lying on the floor, and a black frown darkened his face.

'He rang again.' As before, it wasn't a question but a statement. 'I told you not to answer the phone!' he exploded when Catherine nodded.

'But it could have been Dad—or Ellie!' Catherine protested. It had seemed a thoroughly reasonable argument earlier; now, faced with the furious glare of his disapproval, she saw her actions as hopelessly foolish.

'And it could have been Joe—which it was!'

'Well, yes.'

What had she expected? Comfort? Sympathy? Soft, soothing words? If she had dreamed of any such thing, then she had been very swiftly disillusioned. Catherine shifted uneasily from one foot to the other, the burning force of Evan's anger seeming to scorch over already tightly strung nerves, and she couldn't help feeling very much like some naughty schoolgirl being reproved by a sternly critical headmaster.

'How many times do I have to say this, Catherine?' Evan sighed his exasperation as he pushed one hand roughly through the darkness of his hair. 'You can't trust anyone!'

'But *Ellie*—she's a friend! You can't mean—'

A look into his hard, set face, stilled the protest in her throat.

'She might be the best friend you've got, but you can't afford to take any risks,' Evan returned with brutal determination. 'Think about it, Cat,' he added as she still looked mutinous, her mouth drawn tight in an expression of rejection of all he said, her blue eyes blazing rebellion. 'Last night—that phone call from Joe—when did it happen?'

'Just after—' Her mind reeled as she saw what he was driving at. 'He phoned just after Ellie rang to check I was here. But that was just coincidence! You can't possibly imagine Ellie had anything to do with it!'

'Coincidence or not, it means you have to be very, very careful. Someone has let this bastard know that you're here, and until we know who that someone is we can't afford to take any risks.'

The rational part of Catherine's mind acknowledged the truth of what Evan was saying, but it seemed so extreme—and *Ellie*! Apart from her father, Ellie had been her one rock in all this—someone she could turn to when the pressure got too much. Without her... If she had felt isolated before, now she felt totally desolate.

'Who can I trust?' It was a low, despondent whisper.

'No one,' Evan returned harshly. 'This animal has threatened you with actual physical harm. Until we sort this out, anyone and everyone could be a potential threat—not just because they might be him, but because, unknowingly or not, they might let him know where you are, what you're doing.'

'Even you?'

The turquoise eyes were turned on her, the steady, narrow-eyed gaze unnerving.

'What do you think?'

She didn't know how to answer him; could only shake her head despairingly. The intense relief she had felt such a short time before at seeing him return seemed to have evaporated, disappeared completely, and she didn't know where to turn.

'But one thing you can be sure of,' Evan continued quietly, 'I promised I'd stay to the end of this, and I always keep my promises. I may have had to go out today, but that was a mistake. It won't happen again—you have my word on that. I'm not letting you out of my sight again.'

'Is that a promise or a threat?' Catherine's voice was shaky, her attempt at laughter unconvincing even in her own ears.

'Take it whatever way you want to,' Evan returned, his voice hard and emotionless. 'Just be sure of one thing. Until this Joe is caught and put away, I'm not moving from your side—even if you beg me to go.'

CHAPTER SIX

'Now, Cathy, darling, are you *sure* you're going to be all right? I could always—'

'I'll be fine, Dad.'

Catherine was pleased to find that her voice had a ring of conviction; at least she sounded positive, even if she didn't actually *feel* it.

'After all, there hasn't been any more trouble, has there?'

She and Evan had agreed not to tell her father about Joe's latest phone call. If he knew about it, then she was sure that Lloyd would consider cancelling his trip to Japan.

'And I know how important this trip is to you. The Japanese contract will make all the difference in the world. Besides—I have Evan to take care of me.'

She cursed the betraying tremor of her voice on Evan's name that gave away too much of the way she felt about him. Having Evan to protect her was very much a two-edged sword, and even now, after three days in his company, she couldn't decide whether the sense of security that resulted from his presence in her life was worth the hassle of having to put up with him invading her privacy in this way.

'I'm not letting you out of my sight again,' he had said, and over the past weekend he had made it plain that he meant precisely what he had said. He had stuck to her side like glue, it seemed she couldn't move, couldn't even breathe without looking up and seeing those cold sea-green eyes fixed on her, watching, assessing, observing every action, every gesture so closely

83

that she almost felt he might be able to see into her mind and read her thoughts.

Only at night, in bed, could she escape. Only in the hours of darkness, alone in her room, did she have any peace from his persistent, watchful presence.

'That's your cases in the car.'

Catherine started as the object of her thoughts came into the hall from outside and tossed the car keys to her father.

'It's time you were off if you don't want to miss your plane.'

'We were just coming.'

Catherine struggled to ignore the prickling sensation of uneasy awareness that always troubled her when Evan was near, lifting the tiny hairs on the back of her neck in the instinctive reaction of a wary cat faced with an unwelcome intruder into its territory.

'I'll see you to the car, Dad.'

'No.'

Evan's hand shot out, fastening bruisingly around her upper arm, just below the short sleeve of her white cotton shirt, worn with the inevitable jeans.

'Not you,' he added emphatically when she turned a mutinous face towards him. 'You stay indoors.'

For a moment Catherine considered rebelling, but then she abandoned the idea as foolhardy. For one thing, she knew he was right—it would be stupid to advertise her presence here—and for another, she had little hope of being able to free herself from Evan's grip which, while not actually painful, was hard enough to warn her that with very little effort he could change it into something far less controlled.

'Evan's right, Dad.' She forced a smile even though her teeth were clenched tightly against the urge to shake off that restraining hand. 'We don't know who might be watching.'

But to remind her father of the danger was a mistake. His face clouded, a frown creasing his forehead.

'Perhaps I should stay—'

'Oh, no, Dad—you can't! If you don't get this contract, you'll have to seriously consider laying people off, and I'd hate to think of anyone losing their job because of me.'

'I know you'll think that I'm fussing unnecessarily.' Lloyd turned to Evan. 'But Cathy's all I have. After Melissa left—'

'Dad,' Catherine cut in, uncomfortable at the thought of her father exposing the messy family history to Evan's coolly assessing scrutiny, 'it's getting late...'

'And you have nothing to worry about,' Evan assured him. 'I'll see that no harm comes to Catherine. You have my word on that.'

And he always kept his word, Catherine reflected. He had told her that, and—

At that point her thought processes blew a fuse as Evan's punishing grip on her arm changed into a casual but inescapable arm slung round her waist, apparently easily friendly, but in reality drawing her hard against the warm strength of his body and holding her there when she would have stiffened and moved away.

'I'll guard her with my life,' he assured the older man, and the deep, husky sincerity in his tone combined with the intensely physical awareness that sizzled through her body, seeming to strike sparks at the connection of arm and hip and thigh, to create a disturbingly heady mixture that made her head swim as if she had just downed a tumblerful of the most potent brandy.

Through the red haze that filled her mind she was vaguely aware of her father saying goodbye, his words touched with a note that, when taken with the look in his eyes, left her in no doubt that he had noticed Evan's action, and had interpreted it as meaning that their relationship had moved on past the strictly business level it had started out on.

It took every ounce of self-control she possessed to remain still in Evan's hold until the door had closed behind Lloyd and his car had sped off down the drive. Then, wrenching herself free, she rounded on him furiously, blue eyes sparking with anger.

'And just what was all that in aid of? ''I'll guard her with my life''!' She echoed his words with cynical mockery. 'I thought I told you to keep your hands to yourself. I said I didn't want you mauling me—'

She broke off abruptly, his, 'I never *maul*,' seeming to hang in the air between them.

'But you wanted your father to go on this trip,' Evan put in quietly.

'Of course I did. But—'

'He wasn't going to leave. I could see that in his eyes. I had to do something to convince him that you were safe with me.'

So he had used her again, in the same calculated way as before.

'Implying that we had a—a relationship!'

One corner of Evan's mouth quirked up in wry amusement at her tone, and in spite of herself she found that one foolish, irrational part of her brain had registered the electrically charged attraction of that boyish response.

'Suggesting that things were—developing—between us,' he agreed. 'It seemed the best way to convince him that I would care for you as much as he would—and it worked.'

'I suppose it did,' Catherine conceded grudgingly, having to admit, if only to herself, that Evan's deception had had the desired effect. At least her father would be able to go off on his business trip with a peaceful mind— even if that peace was based on a totally false impression.

'Why so peeved, Cat? You surely aren't disappointed? Could it be that you wanted my—*mauling*—' he emphasised the word with deliberate mockery '—to be real. Is *that* what you wanted?'

'Certainly.not!' Catherine flung the rebuttal at him, raising her voice emphatically as much to drown out the echoes in her head as to convince him that she meant what she said.

'Is this what you want,' he had said on that first day in his room, when he had used the sensual appeal of his touch, his kisses, as coldly and deliberately as he had used the apparent gesture of affection just now. And the terrible thing was, while she had been unable to stop herself from responding, to him it had meant nothing; it was just something he could switch on and off at will, without concern for how it made her feel.

'You really are an arrogant bastard! How dare you assume—?'

'Assume? I assumed nothing, Cat. I was just trying to find out exactly what you wanted from me.'

'What I want—' goaded beyond endurance by his mocking tone, Catherine forced the words out from between clenched teeth '—is for you to realise once and for all that you're here for one reason, and one reason only, and that is to protect me from this animal who's stalking me. I'll thank you to remember that, and get it through your thick skull that anything else—any more of your unwanted and repellent attentions to me—is the last thing on my mind. It makes my skin crawl.'

Not true, a tiny voice inside her head protested, reminding her of the nights she had lain awake, sleep eluding her completely as she fought to stop her wanton thoughts from straying to the disturbing recollection of how it had felt to be in Evan's arms, how his kisses had awoken a hunger deep inside, how his caresses had fed that need as dry tinder fuelled a fire.

She had been lying to herself when she had thought that only in bed was she free of Evan. Even there, in the sanctuary of her own room, her peace was invaded by dark, sensual, unwanted and uncontrollable thoughts that made her blood run hot in her veins and had her twisting restlessly in an agony of frustrated yearning.

'My, we do overreact, don't we?' Evan drawled. 'All I did was put an arm around you. Just one little touch and you go up in flames—like a keg of gunpowder into which someone's dropped a lighted match.'

'I did not—'

Catherine caught herself up sharply, painfully aware of the old saying about protesting too much. She was sure it was in Evan's mind too; she could practically read the words in the taunting expression in those deep aquamarine eyes.

'You took me by surprise.' She changed tack hastily, hoping that the coolness of her tone would convince him, though painfully aware of the fact that she wasn't even convincing herself. 'And I'm sorry if I overreacted. I'm very much on edge all the time. It's not knowing—having to think before I do anything—always being afraid that the phone will ring. And it makes it all so much worse not knowing a thing about him—not even what he looks like.'

The catch in her voice was not artifice. She had abandoned all pretence now, her blue eyes shadowed and dark, the angry colour that had washed her cheeks fading rapidly.

'I keep imagining all these horrors...'

'I know. Oh, Cat, I know how hard it must be for you.'

The gentleness of Evan's voice shocked her. It was in such contrast to the unyielding hardness, the dark mockery he had used before. To her consternation his change of attitude hit home with a force that rocked her already precarious grip on her composure, bringing hot tears to her eyes so that she had to bite down hard on her lower lip to stop them falling.

'I remember I once went to a production of *Macbeth* where there was no scenery, no props—just the audience's imagination. In the scene where they bring on Macbeth's head, the images that people created in their own minds were far worse than anything any special effects department could put together, because we all imagined our worst fears. So I can guess how it must be for you. But I won't let him get to you, I promise. I'll keep you safe—you don't have to worry while I'm here.'

It was happening again. That disturbing, weakening sensation was creeping over her, making her feel that she was losing all control over the situation. At moments like this she would willingly have put herself entirely into Evan's hands; put her safety, her future, her hopes and dreams into his power to do with as he pleased. And if he chose to destroy her she would not have the strength to resist.

'I'll keep you safe,' he had said, but he only meant that he would protect her from Joe. Physically, he would keep her secure. But what about the emotional risks inherent in this situation? Who would defend her from the threat that Evan himself posed?

'Come on, let's not brood on things.' Evan was obviously determined to change her mood. 'Tell me, what would you like to do today?'

'Do?' Catherine felt as if she was dragging herself back from a long way away, her mind still chilled by the fear that had gripped it. 'I can't do anything—I can't go out.'

'Don't be a defeatist,' Evan reproved. 'I've said I'll look after you. You can't hide away all your life—that would mean this bastard's won. So, come on, what would you most like to do—within reason—if you had the choice?'

'You mean it?' It had been so long since she had just been able to go out, do ordinary things. 'Well—'

A tiny smile surfaced.

'Do you know what I'd really like? Some clothes—my clothes! I'm sick and tired of wearing the same jeans and T-shirts. It's hot. I want to put on a dress—shorts. Please can we go to my flat and get me something to wear?' The look she turned on him was bright-eyed, pleading.

'How like a woman!' Evan's laughter was a warm, rich sound, easing the bruised feeling round her heart. 'I should have known—offer her the world and she chooses clothes.'

This time his teasing had no bite. His amusement was genuine, and she was able to return his smile without any of the uneasy feelings that had previously troubled her.

'Believe me, if you'd worn the same pair of jeans and alternated a couple of T-shirts for almost the past fortnight, you'd want a change as much as I do. It's not vanity but sheer boredom.'

'All right, I believe you.' His smile was wide, devastatingly so, and Catherine felt its impact from the tingling top of her head right down to where her toes curled on the carpet in hidden response. 'When do you want to leave?'

'As soon as possible. Just give me a couple of minutes—I have some bits of washing that I put in the machine last night and I'd like to hang them out on the line, then we can be off.'

'Well, if someone had told me, I'd never have believed it!'

Evan stood in the middle of the living-room of Catherine's flat and stared round him, a bemused expression on his face. Watching him, Catherine couldn't suppress a cheeky smile at his expense.

'Not quite what you expected, hmm?'

'Not at all.' Evan sounded distracted, his attention still on his surroundings. But then he caught sight of her expression and rounded on her in mock indignation. 'Well, it's hardly La Maison Davies, is it?'

'La Maison *Lloyd* Davies,' Catherine corrected pertly. '*This* is Chez Catherine—a different matter entirely.'

'You can say that again.'

Evan moved over to the shelves by the window, his big hands sorting gently through the collection of shells arranged above an assortment of books.

'And what does your father think of all this?'

'Oh, he hates it.' Catherine's gesture encompassed the clutter of books and records, the brightly coloured wall-hangings, collected from different countries she had visited, more china cats on a specially constructed shelf. 'After all, his own style is so elegant, so understated—so minimal.'

'I thought you shared his taste until I saw your bedroom.'

'Most people do.' Catherine's voice was slightly jerky. The sense of invasion she had felt when he had gone into her room still lingered at the back of her mind. 'I expect it's something to do with looking so much like Dad.'

'You both have the same cool colouring—pale eyes, pale hair. It gives an impression of being unapproachable, somehow—withdrawn—almost fey.'

For a long moment the sea-coloured eyes met hers, suddenly dark and unreadable.

'You can seem like one of those images of a mermaid sitting on a rock, combing her long fair hair and enticing sailors to their destruction—the sort of thing you see in books of fairy stories.'

'Is that how you see mermaids—as dangerous forces? I've always thought of them more like the Little Mermaid in the story by Hans Christian Andersen—you know, the one who gave up the sea for love, who wanted human legs in order to be perfect for her prince, but when she was given them they hurt so terribly that it was agony for her to walk.'

'And he didn't really love her either, if I remember rightly. He married someone else and she died of a broken heart.'

'Only because she couldn't bring herself to harm the man she loved. The witch gave her a knife and told her to stab it into the prince's heart. When his blood touched her feet they would turn back into her fish's tail and she could go back to her life in the sea. But she couldn't bring herself to do it.'

'So she died rather than let the man she loved come to any harm.' Evan made a faint grimace. 'And these are the stories we read to our children to send them to sleep!'

'Could you do that?' Catherine asked suddenly, impulsively, driven by the need to distract herself from disturbing images of Evan reading a bedtime story to a young child—his child. 'Sacrifice your happiness for someone else, I mean.'

For a long drawn-out moment she thought he wasn't going to answer, but then he drew in a deep breath and picked up one particularly lovely shell—a swirling coil of peachy-beige—turning it over and over in his strong fingers, his eyes on his hands, his gaze slightly unfocused.

'If I loved someone, I wouldn't think twice. I'd do anything on God's earth rather than see her hurt. If she was the one, then, yes—I'd give my life for her.'

There was no bravado in the way he spoke. It was no macho declaration, but a calm and quiet statement, and all the more convincing because of that. Something twisted deep inside Catherine's heart at the sincerity and conviction of that 'I'd give my life', and she couldn't help contrasting it with the more cynically motivated way he had told her father he would protect her with his life.

'If I loved someone...' Evan had said. Clearly, he hadn't yet found the right woman, but when he did...

She was suddenly a prey to a bitter sense of envy towards the woman who might one day win this man's heart, earn that heartfelt devotion, and she couldn't help wondering if she would ever inspire such a feeling in anyone in the future. Only if she could would she be able to commit herself to marriage. With her parents' example before her, she wasn't likely to risk anything otherwise.

'There's a shell there from every beach I've ever visited in my life.'

She spoke simply to break the silence that had fallen. Coming to his side, she selected a shell and picked it up.

'This one's from Spain—and that's from Malta. This comes from Wales. Oh, and this one...'

Her face softened, her lips curving into a warm smile.

'This is from a small place called Sandymount, just outside Dublin. I went there when I was just five.'

'You obviously have very happy memories of that holiday.'

'Mmm.' Catherine touched the tiny shell lightly and sighed. 'It was the last time we were all together as a family.'

'Before your mother left?' Evan questioned softly, bringing her head round sharply. 'Your father still seems to be carrying something of a torch for her.'

'I suppose he is.' She aimed for indifference, but only managed to achieve a brittle coldness that made her wince inwardly. 'Now I'd better get on—pack some clothes.'

'There's no rush.' To her relief, Evan accepted her attempt to change the subject. 'Why don't I make us both a drink while you open your post?'

He nodded to the bundle of letters lying on the table where he had dropped them after picking them up from the doormat on their arrival.

She had been deeply appreciative of the fact that he was with her then, she recalled, grateful for the way he had judged her feelings intuitively, sensing without a word having to be spoken the way her mood had changed as she approached her front door. He had been aware of the nervousness that had descended as the sight of the familiar surroundings awoke memories of those terrifying phone calls, the letters, the parcels.

Perhaps the cruellest thing that the stalker had done was to make her feel so afraid in her own home, and somehow Evan had sensed that, taking the key from her hand as she'd hesitated, opening the door and going in ahead of her to check that all was safe before he had allowed her to set foot over the threshold.

'Would you like tea or coffee—or something cool?' Evan was on his way to the kitchen.

'Something cold, I think. If you look in the fridge, there should be some elderflower cordial. That would be lovely mixed up with sparkling water and some ice. Perfect on a day like this.'

She was flicking through the small pile of letters as she spoke, wrinkling her nose in distaste at what she found.

'There's nothing here worth bothering with—just bills, junk mail, a bank statement and—*Evan!*'

He was at her side in an instant, reacting with swift instinctiveness to the change in her voice. The blue envelope lay where she had dropped it as she froze into shocked stillness.

'It's from him,' she managed shakily. 'I recognize the handwriting—and he always uses that colour paper.'

Strong, warm arms came round her, powerful hands grasped her shoulders as she stared at the small rectangle as if it was some deadly poisonous snake.

'All right, Cat, I'll deal with it. No, don't touch it.' Firm fingers stilled her hand when she would have reached out again. 'Let's try and keep any fingerprints intact—though by that time it's been through various postal sorting offices and a couple of delivery men, I don't suppose there's too much to find. But we'll hand it over to the police anyway. Have you got a plastic bag I can put it in?'

'Kitchen cupboard by the sink—top shelf.'

Catherine spoke like an automaton, her whole attention fixed on the envelope. It seemed to hold her transfixed, unable to move or look away.

'Sometimes I forget about him, you know,' she said drearily, unable to lift her voice above a flat monotone that revealed her sense of shock more than any frantic hysteria. 'For days—a whole week, even—nothing happens, and I begin to hope—to think that maybe he's given up—got bored—left the country—anything. But then something like this will happen.'

She watched as Evan manoeuvred the letter into the polythene bag, carefully avoiding touching it, before folding the protective cover over it and sliding it into the pocket of his black linen jacket.

'I should take that to the police—'

'You leave that to me. I'll take care of it. Now, how about that drink?'

It was almost as if the letter had cast a spell over her, and now that it was out of sight its power was broken, freeing her again. Or was it the result of her relief at knowing that Evan was there, that whatever happened he would cope? Either way, Catherine suddenly found that she could move again, that her stiffly frozen mouth could smile—which she did, brightly, straight into Evan's face.

'What was that for?' Just for a second he had looked almost shaken, his head going back sharply.

'To say that I'm glad you're here.'

'Well, thanks.' His smile showed that he had recovered his composure, was once more his calm, controlled self. 'I'm glad I'm here too,' he added, with a soft intensity that made her insides twist painfully so that, suddenly fearful of what her eyes might reveal to him, she turned away hastily.

'I'll get the drinks.'

'No.' Evan's voice was firm. 'You've had a fright—you need to recover. Sit down—I'll get the drinks.'

'I don't need to sit down!' Catherine protested, but the words had a shake in them, and she couldn't find the strength to resist as Evan manoeuvred her into a chair and disappeared into the kitchen, reappearing a short time later with a couple of tall glasses in which ice clinked appealingly.

'Mmm, that was delicious!' Catherine sighed after a long refreshing drink. 'Keep this up, and perhaps I'll forgive all your bossiness and bullying.'

'Not bullying, Cat,' Evan put in, once more using the quiet, soft voice that did disturbing things to her ability to think clearly. 'Someone has to make sure that you take a few basic precautions—for your own good.'

'I can look after myself!' Catherine protested. 'I was managing fine. All right then, not *fine*,' she amended, interpreting the sceptical look he threw at her, 'but I would have coped.'

She was backpedalling desperately, trying to recover from the revealing admission of moments before, and to judge from Evan's expression he knew exactly what was going through her mind.

'I'm sure you're a very independent lady, Cat, but—'

'Don't call me that!' Unease pushed her into unwary speech. 'My name is *Catherine*, and I'd prefer it if you use it correctly.'

To her consternation, Evan simply shook his head. 'I prefer Cat,' he drawled lazily. 'It suits you better.'

'Suits me? In what way?' In spite of herself she was intrigued, though the grin that lit up his face warned her that she wasn't going to like his reply.

'Well, everyone knows that a cat is one of the most beautiful creatures on earth—all silky fur and glowing eyes, and possessed of a devastating sensuality...'

Pausing, deliberately she was sure, he reached for his glass and drained it thirstily, those changeable eyes watching her over the rim of the glass. With an effort, Catherine held herself back from adding the enquiring, But? Because there was a but to follow—she was sure of that—but she wasn't going to let herself be provoked into using it. To do so would be to fall into his carefully laid trap.

She was right.

'Though, of course, with even the most relaxed and gentle-looking of felines, it pays to be a little cautious. Because you never know just when they might unsheathe their claws and scratch.' Deep in that aquamarine gaze was a glint of wicked amusement. 'Hard.'

Carefully Catherine schooled her features into an expression that was as unrevealing as possible. It wasn't quite as difficult as she might have anticipated because, if the truth were told, she couldn't really have explained her reaction—even to herself.

She didn't know which disturbed her most—the comment about her tendency to lash out, verbally, or Evan's earlier description of a cat, and by association of herself. Did he really mean that in his view *she* possessed glowing eyes and—what was it he had said?—a devastating sensuality?

'You asked,' Evan said drily, the amusement that still lurked at the back of his eyes making them dangerously attractive.

'So I did.' Ruthless control tightened her voice.

Following his example, she emptied her glass and set it down on the table with a decisive click.

'I think it's time I collected those clothes,' she said, getting to her feet. 'We don't want to hang around here all day.'

She thought she would be left to the privacy of her room, hearing Evan get up and go into the kitchen to rinse out the glasses, but she had barely had time to select a few items, folding them carefully into a small case, before he was back, lounging in the doorway, observing her with cool, clear eyes.

Catherine was so aware of that watchful gaze that every movement seemed to be emphasised, exaggerated, her tension growing and her heart seeming to beat in an uncomfortable, irregular rhythm. She had to fight against the urge to demand to know whether he had to watch her quite so closely.

She was already coming to know that Evan Lindsay was a man who did things by his own rules, and that to question his actions was one sure way of making him all the more determined to carry them through. So she forced herself to ignore his watchful presence, concentrating so fiercely on her task that she jumped when he spoke to her.

'This room is so typical of the rest of your flat, in its use of colour and design, that I can only assume it's very much *not* Lloyd too. So where does this very different sort of taste come from? Is it a characteristic inherited from your mother?'

Catherine stiffened, her hand suddenly still on the shirt she was folding. She kept her eyes fixed on the green cotton as she answered unwillingly.

'My mother left when I was barely five.'

'I know—but that doesn't mean that you're not at all like her. Physically, you're obviously very much Lloyd's daughter, but she must have had some input somewhere—some contribution to your make-up.'

'I doubt it.' Catherine's voice was coolly distant, and she made herself go to the wardrobe and select a couple of dresses, deliberately not looking at Evan. 'And even if any part of me did come from her, I didn't know her well enough to be aware of it.'

'But surely—?'

'Mr Lindsay—' the formality of the name was used with deliberate coldness '—you may be in charge of my safety, but that is all. My private life is none of your business, and I'll thank you to keep well out of it. The subject is closed.'

She hadn't really expected him to accept her declaration without argument, and so was frankly amazed when he simply shrugged his shoulders and straightened up, stretching lazily.

'Whatever you say, dear Cat. Is that the lot?' he nodded towards the case lying on the bed.

'No.' Smarting from the double-edged 'Cat'—which was how he had meant it, she was sure—Catherine wanted to assert herself, in however small a way. 'I want one or two—'

But Evan didn't let her finish.

'This is a security operation, not a Monte Carlo holiday,' he cut in sharply. 'What you've packed already will do fine.'

And with a swift, brusque movement he slammed the lid of her case shut, snapping closed the catches before lifting it and carrying it from the room, leaving her with no alternative but to follow.

'But—'

'But nothing, Catherine,' Evan flung over his shoulder at her. 'We've been here long enough. Any longer and your friend Joe will probably realise where you are. If you want to hang around and wait for him to phone, then...'

But of course he didn't have to complete the sentence; just the thought was enough to have Catherine hurrying after him.

'All right. I get the point! I'm coming.'

...

CHAPTER SEVEN

BEING with Evan was like discovering that the path you had been following through life had suddenly turned into an emotional roller coaster—all peaks and troughs, Catherine reflected as the car turned into the drive of her father's house some time later. It seemed that ever since she had first met him she had spent her time seeming to go up towards some sort of rapport at one moment, only to plummet down hard the next, with the sickening sensation of having left her stomach behind.

The journey back from her flat had been accomplished in an uncomfortable silence, one that had drawn her nerves so tight that she had feared they might actually snap under the strain of sitting still at Evan's side, pretending that she couldn't care less while in fact her insides were churning in a nauseating response to his abrupt change of mood.

She knew that she had only herself to blame. She had deliberately provoked him, slapping him down like that—and earning herself the use of that ambiguous nickname as a reproof—but telling herself that didn't help matters, or ease the prickling sense of irritation at the way he had overruled her.

'Here you are, safely home again.'

'Obviously.'

She knew the tartness had been a mistake as soon as she spoke, and cursed her foolishness in not thinking before she had opened her mouth, but her already edgy feeling had been complicated by the fact that during the silent journey her body seemed to have developed a will of its own and, in contrast to the hostility of her thoughts, had suddenly become hypersensitive to Evan sitting so close to her in the confined space of the car.

Every movement of his hands, strong and capable on the steering wheel, the tension of the muscles in his legs as he changed gear, the sound of his breathing, the scent of his aftershave, even the warmth of his skin seemed to reach out like soft, tantalising fingertips, brushing across nerves already sensitised and exposed and awakening them to a sexual awareness that was all the more devastating because it was unconscious and unwilling. Suddenly the car seemed too small, too confining, Evan's powerful body far too close. She *had* to get out.

She was clutching the doorhandle, wanting to wrench it open, when Evan's hand closed over hers, strong fingers stilling her nervous movement.

'Not yet.' His voice was soft, but a note of hard authority underlined the fact that she would be foolish to resist.

'Why?'

Rational common sense told her that she would be wise to heed the warning, but a spark of defiance made her already uneasy frame of mind flare into an explosion of resistance that blew away the more sensible reaction.

'I want to get out! I'm hot and thirsty and—and I can't stay in this car a moment longer.'

It was worse than before because now the flesh of her arm seemed to scorch in response to his touch, and sensations like the burning response of an electric shock seared over every nerve, making her want desperately to twist away.

'Not yet,' Evan repeated obdurately. 'Have some sense, Cat. We've been out all morning. At least let me check the place out before you blunder in, disturbing God knows what.'

'Disturbing...'

All the fight went out of Catherine at once, leaving her feeling limp as a pricked balloon, a cold, creeping sensation slithering down her spine and making her shiver in fearful response.

'Do you really think...? Or are you just trying to frighten me?'

'Not to frighten—just to make you see sense.'

The hard fingers released her at last, and she had to struggle against the urge to rub at her arm where she was sure his grip had marked her.

'Come on, Cat, surely you can see that it's wiser for you to wait here until I've given the place the once-over—made sure everything's safe.'

Catherine could only nod silently, unable to persuade her tongue to form any words in reply, her worried blue gaze going to the elegant frontage of her father's house, seeing it no longer as the place where she had grown up, where there had always been a warm welcome for her—even after she had moved into her own flat—somewhere where she had always been so *safe*. Now it seemed that its familiar walls might conceal a threat that blighted her life, destroying all sense of security.

'Damn him!' Blind anger and distress almost choked her. 'Is he going to taint everything that I love?'

'Only if you let him,' Evan said quietly. 'And not if I have anything to do with it. Wait here and I'll give you a call if everything's OK.'

When he smiled at her like that she was instantly back on the roller coaster, Catherine thought, watching from the safety of the locked car as he strode towards the house, turning at the door to give her a small, encouraging wave before he disappeared inside.

With that glow in his eyes, and the hard, set features softened so dramatically, she could almost feel herself soaring up, up, above the clouds, glorying in the sense of delight and freedom, escaping from all the fear and anxiety that was such a burden to her. The problem was the equally swift and far more devastating descent that she knew awaited her just at the very peak of the experience.

Where was Evan? How long did it take to check the house? Surely he should be back by now. But what if...?

Her mind was suddenly flooded with images from every thriller movie she had ever seen, of men with guns sidling up to the door of a room and flinging it open, bursting through the doorway, revolver held at arm's length.

Did *Evan* have a gun?

The thought drew her up short, staring sightlessly through the windscreen, once more brought up hard against just how little she knew of this man. She knew that he was determined, resourceful—ruthless. After all, she'd seen that heartlessness turned against herself. But was he capable of violence?

He was army-trained, and she believed he could carry out anything that required cold-blooded determination and strength. He was capable of deliberate manipulation and conniving too, she recalled, with a bitter taste in her mouth. But could he actually hurt another human being?

Oh, where *was* he?

The crime story images intensified in her mind, growing more lurid with every second that passed. She would have heard a shot if one had been fired, she told herself. But what if someone had been waiting—hiding behind a door or a curtain, armed with a knife or a club? What if Evan was lying unconscious?

'Evan!'

Not pausing to think, acting purely instinctively, she pushed open the car door.

'Oh, my God, no! Evan—'

It seemed to take an age to reach the house, but then she was at the door, her breath coming in raw, painful gasps as she pushed it open.

'Evan—please!'

The house was strangely silent, frighteningly so. Surely she should be able to hear *something*!

'Oh, God! Evan—please!'

'What the hell—?'

Footsteps sounded on the landing, heavy, masculine footsteps, and then a figure appeared at the top of the stairs. For one appalling second her eyes blurred so that she couldn't make out anything beyond the fact that it was big and dark and forcefully male, but then her vision cleared and, thankfully, reassuringly, she saw that Evan was coming towards her, long legs dealing with the stairs two or three at a time.

'Oh, Evan! Thank God!'

'What is it? Cat—what the hell's wrong?'

He was at her side and had caught her up in his arms, and it felt fiercely, wonderfully comforting to be there, with his strength used to protect and reassure, not to hurt.

'What *is* it?' he demanded harshly when she was too overcome to speak.

'Oh, Evan! I thought something terrible had happened. I thought that you—' She could only shake her head to express the horror she had imagined.

'You thought—? Oh, Cat.'

The catch in his voice communicated itself to Catherine even through the slowly receding panic that was still clouding her mind, bringing her down to earth with a bump. She blinked hard, staring up into his face and seeing, devastatingly, the amusement that gleamed in his eyes.

'You're laughing!'

Recoiling violently, she wrenched herself from his arms, blue eyes flashing fire that was a mixture of fury and pain—and even she would not have been able to separate the different elements to say in what proportions they were combined.

'It isn't *funny*! I was scared and you're laughing at me!'

'Oh, Cat...' It was the voice he might have used to calm a nervous thoroughbred, and even that double-edged 'Cat' sounded soft and gentle used in this way. 'I'm not laughing at you—at least, not at your fear—but at the thought of you rushing in like that, like a mother tiger with her claws out, coming to *my* rescue.'

Reaching out gently, he took her hand as he spoke, and if she needed any reinforcement of what he was saying, their linked fingers gave it to her. Where hers were long and fine, the skin white and delicate, the nails softly oval and touched with a pale pink polish, his hands were strong and square, the powerful fingers topped with uncompromisingly short, blunt nails.

She knew the power of those hands, had felt it on her skin, a foretaste of the potential impact of which the muscular body was capable if it was fully unleashed. Just the thought of it woke such a sensual response in her that she couldn't control the shiver of longing that shook the slender length of her body.

'Oh, hell—I'm sorry! You're obviously shocked. Look, come into the kitchen and let me get you a drink.'

Catherine didn't know whether to be relieved or disturbed by the way that Evan had obviously misinterpreted the reason for her reaction, and she found herself incapable of either responding or resisting as, still with his hands in hers, he led her into the kitchen.

She was weak enough to admit that she didn't want him to let go, that she drew a degree of strength from his touch that drove away her earlier fears, gave her back her self-control and some calmness of mind. She didn't allow herself to admit, even in the privacy of her own thoughts, to the purely physical pleasure that set her blood singing as the result of his closeness. She would think about that later, she told herself. Right now, she was content simply to let it happen.

'What would you like to drink?' Evan asked when he had installed her on one of the high wooden stools at the breakfast bar. 'Something cold again, or...'

'Isn't hot, sweet tea supposed to be the best thing for shock?' Catherine managed, praying that he would believe the shake in her voice was from the lingering effects of that particular emotion, and not the sudden sense of loss that ripped through her as he left her side.

'Do you *like* sweet tea?'

The frank disbelief in his voice was combined with a wicked, teasing, sidelong glance slanted at her, amusement gleaming in the sea-green depths of his eyes, and the shared moment had her giggling in response, her laughter a response to the release from the constraint she had felt only moments before.

'Yeuch!' She twisted her face into a grimace of distaste. 'I'm not keen on tea anyway; I much prefer coffee. But milky tea with sugar—no way!'

The warmth of his smile delighted her, and she basked in it as if it had the power of the rays of the sun to touch her body, heating her blood.

'You look like a little girl when you do that—like some three-year-old who's just been told there's cabbage for tea.'

'Is that how you see me? As a three-year-old? Well, thanks very much!' Catherine assumed an expression of mock indignation that didn't match the glint of amusement still lingering in her eyes.

'Well, not so much a three-year-old, but—'

He broke off suddenly, his head turning sharply, turquoise eyes narrowing as he stared out into the garden.

'What is it?' Catherine's happy mood vanished abruptly.

'I thought I saw movement.' His attention was fixed on a spot beyond the kitchen window, every muscle in his big body taut. 'No—there's nothing there. I must have been mistaken.'

But he had drawn Catherine's attention to the garden, and by doing so had alerted her to something that puzzled and then worried her.

'It's gone!'

'What?'

Evan's head snapped round. She had his full attention now.

'What's gone?'

'My washing—look!' The wave of her hand indicated the empty line where her clothes had blown in the breeze before they'd left the house earlier that morning.

'Are you sure? Couldn't Mrs Bentley have brought it in?'

'It's Mrs B's day off and— *Oh!*'

Dashing to the door, she flung it open and then froze, staring down at the pegs that lay spread out over the lawn—pegs that had previously secured her washing.

'Evan!'

At first glance, the litter on the ground had looked purely random, totally haphazard, but now she studied it more closely she saw that in fact it was laid out in a very careful arrangement. There was the unmistakable shape of an H—an O...

'Honey!'

Behind her, she heard Evan's voice speak her thoughts.

'Catherine, precisely what did you hang out on the line?'

Catherine. If she had needed it, the use of her full name would have been enough to alert her to his change of mood. The laughing light-heartedness of moments before was gone for good.

'My underwear,' she said, her heart clenching on a mixture of fear and a terrible sense of loss for the destruction of what they had shared. Joe had struck again, destroying her peace of mind at a stroke. And this time it seemed so much worse, because for a very short space of time she had forgotten just who Evan was and why he was here, and had been able to react to him simply as a woman to an attractive man.

'Right, that's it—we're out of here. Now.'

The relaxed, smiling man had disappeared; in his place was once more the cold, impersonal bodyguard. It was all Catherine could do not to cry out in distress at the change.

'Cat—*move*!' he snapped. 'You're not flirting with danger now—this is real. If he's been here, he could still be hiding somewhere. I promised your father I'd keep you safe, and I mean to keep that promise.'

'I don't want—'

'You don't have any choice,' Evan declared inimically. 'He's found you. He knows you're here, and he wants you to know it. Do you really want to stay and face him?'

Catherine shuddered at the thought.

'No? Then we're getting out of here *now*. I'll let the police know what's been happening. If we're lucky he'll have left some clue behind while he was out there pinching your knickers. Come on.'

Once more Evan's fingers closed over her hands, but this time in a very different way from the gentleness with which he had held her before. This time, although carefully controlled, his grip had a bruising strength that made her wince, and, looking into his face, she saw stamped onto the hard-boned features such a ruthless determination that her outward flinch matched her mental one.

'Do I have any choice?'

'None at all,' he returned harshly. 'You're coming with me.'

'But I'll need some things...' It all smacked rather too much of out of the frying pan into the fire to go with this man without protest.

'You've got clothes in the car.'

'But where are we going? For how long?'

'For as long as it takes.'

'Then what about washing things—a toothbrush...'

Briefly Evan closed his eyes in an expression of pained exasperation.

'God give me patience! You have two minutes, Cat— just two,' he told her. 'Here—'

Snatching up a plastic carrier bag from the worktop, he thrust it into her hands.

'I suppose I'd better get my things as well, so you can collect what you'll need from the bathroom and I'll see to the bedrooms. *Two minutes*, Cat,' he warned. 'I mean it—and the count starts now.'

He meant it all right; she had no doubt about that. In fact, she was sure he didn't even allow her the full time allocated, because she had barely had time to bundle toothpaste, shampoo and a selection of skin-care into the bag he had given her before he was banging at the bathroom door.

'Time's up, Cat. We're out of here now—in fact, we should have been gone minutes ago. God knows where that bastard is.'

The frightening note in his voice had her rushing out of the bathroom in such haste that she collided with the hard wall of his chest as he stood waiting for her on the landing. The force of the impact knocked her off balance, and she had barely recovered when Evan's hand clamped round her wrist and he pulled her towards the stairs. Even if she had tried to resist, she knew that her struggles would have had no effect—any effort she might make would be ineffectual in the face of his determined power, so she had no option but to go quietly.

If only her mind wouldn't keep throwing up stills from detective films, she thought, on a wave of something very close to hysteria as Evan halted on the doorstep, carefully checking that the coast was clear. It made it all seem so very unreal, so unconnected with *her* somehow, and she had to struggle with an irrational urge to giggle nervously.

'Go straight to the car as quickly as you can,' Evan instructed. 'I'll be right behind you as soon as I've locked up.'

He was as good as his word, slinging his case and another plastic bag on the back seat before sliding into the driver's seat and starting the engine, almost before he was settled.

It was only as the car moved off down the drive at a speed that Catherine privately considered positively suicidal, turning left at the bottom and heading away from town, that some degree of balance returned to her mind, and with it some rational form of thought.

As she watched the familiar streets and landmarks disappear she suddenly felt a twist of apprehension, a clenching of nerves that was made all the worse by a swift, nervous glance at Evan's hard, set profile etched against the car's windows.

'What about the police? You said you'd ring—'

'And I will—but my first priority is to make sure you're safe. I'll give them a call as soon as we arrive.'

'Arrive where?' Her voice came and went unevenly as she recalled that he had ignored the question the first time she had asked it. 'Where are we going?'

'Somewhere where he can't find you. Somewhere he'll never think of looking.'

'And where's that?'

The look Evan turned on her was worryingly blank and unrevealing.

'You'll find out when we get there.'

'But—'

'But nothing, Cat. I'm in charge now, and what I say goes. We're going somewhere where I can look after you, and that's all you need to know. Now, why don't you settle back and get comfortable? We have a long drive ahead of us.'

And after that the subject was closed. The way he turned his attention back to the road, ignoring her attempt at protest, made that only too plain. Unless she tried something very foolish, like trying to snatch the wheel from his hand, she knew she had no option but to do as he said. So she stayed quiet, and even relaxed back in her seat, but her mind was far from calm, racing with fearful, disturbed thoughts.

'Somewhere he'll never think of looking,' Evan had said, and now those words echoed over and over inside of her head, growing more and more ominous with each pounding repetition.

Because if Joe couldn't find her, it was all well and good, but if *she* didn't know where she was going there was no way she could let anyone—her father or her friends—know her destination either.

'You're not flirting with danger now.' Recalling Evan's tone on those words, she shuddered faintly. What was really worrying her was the possibility that, instead of flirting, she had dived head-first into danger with her eyes wide open.

CHAPTER EIGHT

THE sound of the birds singing outside her window woke Catherine the next morning, and as it was a noise that she rarely heard from her bedroom in the flat in central London, she lay still for a few moments, staring sightlessly at the ceiling, trying to work out exactly where she was. Then she remembered and sat up hastily.

She had been so glad to see this room with its cool beige and white colour scheme last night, she recalled, thankful to have reached the end of the long journey. After hours spent on motorways, and what seemed like an age on winding country roads, she had never been so glad to reach her final destination. By then it had been dark and she had been unable to get any idea of her bearings, her only clue being a sign on the side of the road that had welcomed them to a new county.

'Lincolnshire!' she had exclaimed, breaking the silence that had prevailed through the later half of the journey. 'What is there in Lincolnshire?'

Evan had spared her one of those unrevealing, enigmatic glances that had been his only response to any of her questions ever since they had left London.

'A place I know,' he answered cryptically. 'Somewhere where, hopefully, you'll be safe.'

Safe from who? Catherine was tempted to retort, but she bit back the question hastily. If she was going to be stranded in the middle of the English countryside with a man she barely knew, and had no idea how far she could trust, then in this case discretion was definitely the better part of valour.

'And hopefully somewhere I can get a decent meal,' she said instead. 'I'm starving! We've been on the road for hours.'

That at least got through to him, making him glance at the clock on the dashboard and nod agreement.

'Nearly four and half, to be precise. Perhaps it is time we had a break. I'm not at all sure just how much food there'll be at the farm.'

'Am I hearing right?' Catherine deliberately laced her voice with irony in mocking response to his apparent concession. 'Are you really going to let me out of this damn car for more than the three minutes you've allowed me for what is politely called a comfort break?'

'I bought you a cup of coffee,' Evan pointed out with a grin, not in the least fazed by her indignation.

Catherine refused to let herself be swayed by that smile, even though it went straight to her heart with an effect little short of a thudding arrow.

'Oh, yes, you did—and I just love ersatz coffee in a polystyrene cup. Especially when I had to snatch sips at it in between adjusting to the bumps created by travelling at a speed *just* within the legal limit.'

Her sarcasm was more thickly laid on now, and, hearing it, Evan frowned.

'I wanted to get as far away from London as possible— put as much distance between you and that creep as I could.'

His tone said that she should appreciate that fact, and on one very sensible level she did. But with the uncomfortable thoughts that had been in her mind when they had set out still nagging at her she found it impossible to relax back into the unquestioning trust she had previously had in him.

In fact, looking back over the past few days, she found it hard to believe that she had been foolish enough to go along with him so easily. It was one thing to agree. to her father's suggestion that Evan should act as a sort of bodyguard—a minder—while she was in the London house with friends, neighbours and familiar surroundings all around, quite another to be heading off to God knew where without any sort of guarantee of his honesty.

'But no one knows where I am.' It made her stomach clench painfully just to say the words.

'And that's how it should be. You tell no one, you understand—*no one*.'

'But my father—what if he phones the house?'

'He'll know you're with me.'

The intractable arrogance of that declaration combined with Catherine's already volatile state of mind to make her give a crack of brittle laughter that had no trace of humour in it.

'And that's supposed to reassure me?'

Just for a second the speeding car slowed as, in a moment of deliberate silence, Evan turned a swift, assessing glance on her indignant face.

'You don't trust me?' She couldn't interpret what was in his voice, wasn't even sure whether it was a question or not.

'You told me not to!' she flung back.

'So I did.'

His slow smile made her shift uneasily in her seat.

'You're definitely learning,' he murmured, turning his attention pointedly back to the road.

Catherine would never know what had pushed her into the next question. Perhaps it had something to do with the shadowy darkness in the car that obscured Evan's face, making his expression unreadable, or perhaps it was more because they were in transit, so to speak, neither in one place nor another, so that no one could say they were on home ground. Either way, she just knew she couldn't hold back any longer.

'*Can* I trust you?'

This time the silence was longer, and his eyes never left the road.

'What do you think?'

'Obviously I don't know, or I wouldn't have asked the question! Are you going to condescend to answer?' she demanded, when he still left her dangling.

'I don't think it's for me to do that. Only you can decide for yourself, Cat. It's really up to you.'

Which was no help at all—and she was just about to tell him so when, with a sudden, almost shocking change of mood, Evan said lightly, 'There are some services a mile or so ahead—how about stopping there for something to eat?'

'Catherine—Cat? Are you awake?'

Catherine started now as a light tap on the bedroom door intruded into her thoughts. With an effort she dragged herself back to the present.

'Go away!' she growled, unwilling to face Evan while her thoughts were still in such turmoil.

'Oh, come on, Cat! I was just about to offer to make you breakfast. Surely it's about time you were getting up?'

'Why? What would I want to get up for?'

'Because the sun's shining and it's going to be really hot—a perfect day to explore. Don't you want to know more about where you are?'

Privately, Catherine had to admit that she *was* curious about this place to which he'd brought her. She'd hardly seen anything at all last night. Arriving worn out by the travelling, she'd had only a vague impression of winding roads between hedgerows, a long, curving drive and finally the house itself, big and barely visible in the darkness, its unlighted windows blank and somehow unwelcoming.

She had been dead on her feet by the time Evan had unlocked the door and pushed it open, snapping on lights to reveal a wide, wooden-floored hallway that smelled delightfully of beeswax polish and lavender, making her think thankfully that at least wherever he had brought her wasn't neglected and damp.

'Do you want anything to eat or drink?' Evan had asked and she had shaken her head wearily.

'I just want to sleep. Just show me to my room.'

And so he had brought her up here, to this large, cool-looking bedroom, and when he had gone she had been so exhausted that she had only had the energy to strip off her clothes and drape them over a chair before crawling under the soft, downy quilt. Sleep had overwhelmed her almost as soon as her head had hit the pillow.

'Would you like some coffee?' Evan asked from the other side of the door. 'I've got a mug here—'

'*No!*'

Belatedly becoming aware of the fact that, having been too tired even to hunt out a nightdress, she had slept completely naked, Catherine dived back under the covers, pulling them up protectively around her, fearful that he might actually come in.

'I'll have some when I come down.' After all, she could hardly stay in her room all day. It was already...

A swift glance at her watch had her blinking in amazement at the realisation that she had slept most of the morning away and it was already almost eleven. And the thought of breakfast was appealing. As if triggered off by her thoughts, her stomach rumbled emptily, reminding her that the stop at the services had been more than twelve hours ago.

'Give me ten minutes!'

'I'll make that half an hour, shall I?' Evan returned drily. 'In my experience, a woman getting dressed always underestimates the time she'll need.'

'In my case, I mean exactly that!' Catherine refused to let herself think about just what might make up that 'experience'. 'Ten minutes!'

Precisely nine and a half minutes later, showered and dressed in a sleeveless green and white shirt and white shorts—a swift glance out of the window had confirmed Evan's comment that it was going to be a hot day—and with her hair freshly washed, and left loose to dry on her shoulders, she ran lightly down the stairs, drawn by the enticing smell of fresh coffee that wafted up from below.

Reaching the hall, she paused for a moment, looking round her in appreciation at the highly polished wood, its glowing golden tones softly enhanced by the shafts of sunlight that came through the glass panes of the front door, falling in warm pools at her feet. To her right was a huge old pine chest, obviously an antique, that served both as a telephone table and a seat, a brightly coloured tapestry cushion being provided for that purpose. Pausing beside it, Catherine considered, eyeing the telephone thoughtfully.

'Don't even think about it.'

Evan had appeared in a doorway at the far end of the hall, moving surprisingly silently for such a big man.

'You made me jump!' Catherine complained, praying that he would think it was shock that had put the shake into her voice and made hot colour flood her cheeks as a result of the disturbed pounding of her heart—even if she couldn't settle for the more comfortable lie herself. She knew why he had made her jump, and it wasn't just because he had startled her.

It was impossible to deny even to herself the sheer physical impact Evan had on her senses. In well-worn denim jeans, and an immaculately white T-shirt that clung to the tight lines of the powerfully developed muscles of his chest and shoulders, and with the sunlight warming his skin, lighting those changeable eyes and making his dark hair gleam like polished silk, his sensual attraction was lethal to her already vulnerable senses.

Simply looking at him made her nerves tighten in response, her throat suddenly dry so that she had to swallow hard to relieve the uncomfortable feeling.

'And I wasn't thinking of phoning anyone!'

That at least she could declare with enough conviction to make it sound like the truth, though she found it hard to meet those sea-coloured eyes as she moved away from the pine chest and headed for the kitchen.

'So you've finally learned that lesson.'

'Or I'm just playing safe. So what's for breakfast—or I suppose I should say brunch, seeing as it's so late.'

'Eggs, mushrooms, tomatoes—anything you fancy.'

'Great, my mouth's watering already. I— Oh!'

She broke off on a cry of delight, looking round at the pine units, the Aga stove, the terracotta-tiled floor.

'It looks like an old farmhouse kitchen!'

'That's because it is an old farmhouse. How would you like your eggs?'

'Oh—scrambled. With lots of mushrooms—I love them.'

'So do I. And these will be really fresh. Pour yourself some coffee while you're waiting.'

'You've obviously been out, then.'

Catherine tried hard to keep her voice even, but it proved almost impossible. The thought of his going out and leaving her alone, asleep and vulnerable in a strange place, made her stomach twist queasily.

'No, I simply rang the Wilkinsons. They have the working farm.'

Catherine watched with an unwilling fascination as Evan beat eggs and sliced mushrooms, unable to pull her gaze from the confident, efficient movements of his strong, tanned hands.

'Like I said, this is the old farm. It was put up for sale when the family moved into a new, purpose-built house. I promised you I wouldn't leave you alone, Cat,' he added softly, his voice deepening suddenly.

Catherine was intensely thankful that at that moment he turned away to put the eggs into a pan, because she felt that she would have found it impossible to know what sort of expression to wear on her face in response to that last, low-voiced declaration.

She didn't know whether it reassured her or the exact opposite—and even more disconcerting was the ease with which Evan had been able to read the thoughts on her face. His near-telepathic ability in that way made it all the more amazing that she had been able to convince him earlier.

At least she had been telling the exact truth when she had said that she hadn't been thinking of phoning anyone. She had managed that last night, when they had stopped at the services, using the pretext of a visit to the ladies' while leaving Evan to queue for food.

Of course, she hadn't been able to call her father exactly—the practicalities of making an international phone call under such circumstances would have been impossible—but she had managed to snatch a hasty conversation with Ellie, who had promised to pass on to Lloyd the information that his daughter was with Evan and he was not to worry.

'But where *are* you?' her friend had asked, her voice tight with concern.

'To tell you the truth, Ellie, I've no idea. Somewhere in rural Lincolnshire is all I know.'

'With the snarling pit bull, I take it? Cathy, are you sure that's wise?'

'I didn't really have much option in the matter—and my dad did hire him to protect me.'

'Hmm.' Ellie sounded sceptical. 'There's protection and protection, sweetie. Are you sure the guy's not after you for himself? I mean, he seems awfully determined to monopolise you, and you will be pretty isolated...'

Through the plate glass windows of the restaurant, Catherine saw Evan move to the cash desk, and she knew she couldn't risk the possibility that he might look round and see her. She'd already stretched her 'comfort break' to its limit, even allowing for possible queues.

'Evan? Don't you believe it, Ellie. He's made it only too plain that that's not how he sees me.'

It stung to admit it, but there was no room for doubt on that score. Apart from that first morning Evan had kept his distance well and truly, and she knew that his seduction of her—if it could be called that—had had no emotional impulse behind it. It had been cold-blooded and uninvolved in the extreme, meant only to teach her a lesson—which it had done only too well.

'Look, I *have* to go—I'll be in touch again as soon as I can.'

If I can, she thought now, recalling with a faint shiver just how swiftly Evan had reacted to even the suspicion that she might ring someone. A cold, clammy sensation like the slither of melting ice slid down her spine as she was forced to wonder just who was protected most by his determination to keep the rest of the world at bay.

'Here you are—breakfast is served!'

Evan placed a laden plate on the table in front of her, and Catherine made herself pick up her knife and fork, even forcing a smile of acknowledgement. But her earlier appetite had suddenly deserted her, uncertainty and apprehension leaving her feeling distinctly nauseous.

'So tell me about this place.' She forced herself to sound casual and—hopefully—relaxed, even though it was the opposite of the way she was really feeling. 'Who owns it?'

'I do.'

She hadn't expected that. 'But I thought—'

'That I was "just some security man"?'

The sardonic emphasis he put on the last four words left her in no doubt that he was referring back to her conversation with Ellie on the night he had first come to her father's house—dear God, was it only five days ago? She felt as if she had lived through two or three very hectic lifetimes since then.

'Sorry to disappoint you, Cat. If you were expecting a bit of rough—'

'I'm not disappointed! And I was *not* expecting—what you said. I know that you own the company, and even if I didn't I could never think that.'

She would have had to be a fool to dismiss him with such a derogatory description. No one could doubt that Evan's assurance and self-confidence came from a strong sense of his place in the world. He had that indefinable aura of a man who had known success, and expected more of it, and he emanated the undeniable appeal of a vital, supremely masculine sort of energy, the force of which seemed to crackle around him like lightning in a storm-filled sky.

'After all, I sat in on your talks with Dad over the weekend. You must have covered every subject under the sun—books, politics, even opera.'

'*Not* your favourite form of music, as I recall,' Evan put in drily.

'Well, not the ones Dad likes, that's for sure. The sopranos sound like cats being tortured, and I can't make head nor tail of the plots. Perhaps if they were in English it might help.'

'There are some translations— What is it?' he asked, seeing the shocked expression that crossed her face.

'Don't ever let Dad hear you talking like that! As far as he's concerned, opera must only ever be sung in the original language or not at all. To suggest otherwise is nothing short of sacrilege.'

'Well, I'm not such a purist,' Evan laughed. 'If a translation makes a work accessible to more people, I don't have a problem with that. After all, the music still sounds as wonderful.'

'I wish Dad was as open-minded as you. I might actually get to like opera if he was.'

'I have some recordings of English versions you can listen to while you're here, if you like. You could start your education that way, and your father wouldn't know a thing about it.'

'I'd like that.' Catherine suddenly found that her throat muscles had relaxed enough to allow her to contemplate swallowing some of the breakfast Evan had prepared, and she forked up some of the eggs and mushrooms. 'Mmm—this is good!'

'I'm glad to see you eating. You barely touched your meal last night.'

Which was hardly surprising, Catherine reflected. Her stomach had been churning with panic at the thought that he might have seen her on the phone, and the worrying seed of doubt that Ellie had planted in her mind had started to take root there.

'So you do concede that I have more to offer than just being "all brawn and no brain"?'

Almost choking on a bite of toast, Catherine reached hastily for her mug of coffee, swallowing hard to clear her throat. He really must have hearing like a bat if he had caught all of Ellie's comments.

'Look, that was Ellie's opinion, not mine, and she's never met you—so please can't we just forget it? If you knew her you'd realise that she can say the most outrageous things, but she rarely means them.'

Recalling the rest of the conversation she had had with her friend, and what had followed, she went hot and then cold at the memory of Evan's silent, listening presence, and the speed with which he had reacted to cut her off from the other woman.

'And how long have you known this Ellie?'

'Years—almost all my life. As a matter of fact, she was a friend of my mother and father first.'

Catherine's face clouded as she mentally dodged away from the difficult subject of her parents' marriage.

'I met your mother once, you know,' Evan put in quietly, bringing her blue eyes to his face in a rush of surprise. 'Oh, not that I knew it at the time, but your father told me all about her on Saturday night after you'd gone to bed, and I realised that the Melissa Burns I'd seen was the same woman that he'd been married to. It was at a party at my sister's house. She seemed a very glamorous lady.'

'She's certainly that.' Her mother would like Evan, Catherine reflected. She liked men to be 'real' men, and he was definitely that.

'But rather brittle,' Evan continued, startling her. Most men didn't see beyond her mother's golden blonde hair, big blue eyes and voluptuous figure. 'She had a new husband with her—Max someone. Her third?'

'Fourth,' Catherine put in flatly. 'Is your sister in the film world, then?' she asked, intrigued in spite of herself.

'Her husband is—Sam Kingdom, the director.'

'Oh, *that* Sam!'

She didn't know which was uppermost in her mind—shock at the thought that Evan had a brother-in-law who moved in her mother's circles, or the realisation that the Sam he had phoned on Thursday night had actually been *Samuel*.

'Yes, that Sam.' The knowing smile Evan shot her aggravated her inner turmoil. 'Oh, Cat, did you really think I'd break a date with a lady with so little explanation? Believe me, if I had to do that, I'd use rather more finesse.'

Catherine jabbed her knife into the butter with unnecessary force. She hated being so easy to read.

'It's nothing to do with me,' she declared. 'Your private life is none of my business.'

'And what about yours?' Evan shot back softly.

'What?' Catherine could only stare at him in consternation as he pointedly removed the butter dish from her and placed it out of stabbing range.

'I think you've mangled that quite enough. I said, what about *your* private life? Don't you want to know about your mother?'

'Not particularly.' Catherine concentrated fiercely on spreading marmalade on her toast. 'She's not part of my life—private or otherwise.'

'Why not?'

'I would have thought that was obvious. She walked out of my life when I was five. I cried myself to sleep for months, and she broke my father's heart. He's never looked at another woman—not seriously—since then.'

Abruptly she abandoned the toast. She had never really wanted it in the first place.

'Ironical, isn't it? She's on her fourth husband, and Dad hasn't even got over losing her after all these years. At one point I did have a faint hope that he and Ellie ... But it wasn't to be. She married someone else almost a year ago.'

Her tight face softened, her mouth curving into a smile.

'She has a whole new family now—her husband Harry and a couple of grown-up stepsons—Lewis and Geoff.'

'She means a lot to you, doesn't she?'

'I told you, she's a special friend. She looked after me when my mother left. I'd trust her with my life. That's why I won't have you hinting at your nasty little suspicions where she's concerned.'

Evan shrugged off her indignation with a casual gesture.

'They're questions that have to be asked. I might just as well quiz you about past lovers.'

'*What?*'

'Is there any particular man in your past—someone who might have a grudge—anything?'

'I don't know. I can't remember!'

If the truth were told, it seemed as if ever since Evan had come into her life every other man she had ever

known had been wiped from her memory—so much so
that now she found it hard even to think of names, let
alone faces.

'You don't remember?' Something in Evan's tone
grated, making her recall the way he had spoken when
he had talked of her mother.

'Like mother, like daughter—is that what you're
thinking? So many lovers in her past, she can't even remember them?'

'You're putting words into my mouth again.'

His very calmness infuriated her.

'And what about you? How many lovers have *you*
had?'

'*My* love-life isn't relevant here.'

'And mine is?'

'Of course. The man who's stalking you—this so-
called Joe—could be someone from your past. An ex-
lover, someone from whom you parted badly—or it
could be someone who isn't over you, who's let the break-
up fester in his mind.'

It was all perfectly logical and reasonable, but
Catherine felt so tangled up inside that she couldn't bring
herself to admit it.

'It's none of your business! I employed you to protect
me, not to pry into my private life, so I'll thank you to
keep your nose out.'

'You didn't *employ* me to do anything—I volunteered.'

'But my father—' She broke off abruptly as Evan
shook his head with disturbing conviction. 'Dad
didn't—?'

'Like I said, I volunteered. No one's paying me, so
you can't cut off my wages—not that I'd need them.
And as you didn't employ me, you can't sack me either.
I'm in this because I want to be, Cat, whether you like
it or not. And I'm staying—right to the bitter end.'

Would she ever be able to know exactly how she felt
about this man? Catherine wondered dazedly. The roller

coaster had plunged downwards again, more steeply than ever before. In the back of her mind she could hear Ellie's worried voice— 'He seems awfully determined to monopolise you, and you will be pretty isolated...' In despair she shook her head to try and drive it away.

'Is that no, you won't answer my questions, or no, you didn't have a lover who—?'

'It's no, I don't want to continue this conversation!' Catherine got to her feet in a rush, her blue eyes blazing her rejection of his line of questioning.

'These things have to be asked,' Evan stated flatly, rocking her mental balance by adding softly, 'I'd tell you about my past if you asked.'

Catherine's heart clenched in rejection of the honey-toned suggestion. She didn't want to know how many women had shared his life and his bed, couldn't bear to think of him with anyone else—those long, powerful limbs entangled with other, softer ones, that beautiful mouth pressing hot kisses on other lips—the sort of kisses he had given her once, but this time they would be meant, would be used to arouse burning desire in both of them, not just to teach a cold, hard lesson.

'I'm not interested!' she flung at him, her voice high and sharp. 'In fact, I don't want to talk to you at all! And I want to be left alone. I'm going to my room now— I'd be grateful if you'd leave me in peace.'

'Running away?'

Evan's indifference was the last straw. He had turned away, calmly pouring himself another cup of coffee, and Catherine almost gasped aloud as a sensation like the cold slash of an icy knife stabbed deep in her heart, the pain of it bringing bitter tears to her eyes.

'Now you're really making me suspect that you have something to hide,' he said casually.

'On the contrary—' Catherine hid her distress behind the poisonous acidity of her tone '—I'm simply acting on your advice and playing it safe. After all, you were the one who told me not to trust anyone. I mean, how do I know who you are? You could be anyone—even the stalker. Like you said, I don't know who he is, so how do I know he *isn't* you?'

Just for a second Evan looked stunned, his head going back sharply as if she had slapped him hard in the face, something frightening flickering deep in his eyes, but then, disturbingly, he laughed—a harsh, cruel sound, with no trace of humour in it.

'Don't be silly, Catherine.' The coldness in his voice bit into her like acid.

Getting to his feet, he strolled slowly over to her, and it was all Catherine could do not to shrink away fearfully. Summoning all her mental strength, she faced him defiantly.

'So you think I'm friend Joe, do you? Let's see...'

Reaching out a hand, he caught her under the chin, lifting her face and drawing it towards his, oh, so gently.

She tried, her brain screaming commands at her body, but she couldn't make herself resist. It would have been easy to break away—it *should* have been easy—but suddenly it seemed as if nothing worked properly, as if the lines of command between her mind and her limbs had been cut so that she couldn't move. The mesmeric force of those aquamarine eyes, cool and deep and unfathomable, held her transfixed, helpless as a puppet, with no will of her own, only able to act at his command.

'You see, sweetheart, there's one big difference between your twisted admirer and me—and this is it.'

Slowly he bent his head, oblivious to her sharply indrawn breath and the frightened widening of her blue eyes. His mouth touched hers very softly, as lightly as the drift of an autumn leaf falling gently to the ground. It touched, pressed, lingered for barely a moment, and then, just as Catherine felt herself respond helplessly, as she knew the leap of her heart, the sudden warming of her blood, the thrust of need deep inside, he broke the tiny, erotic contact with brutal suddenness, lifting his dark head sharply and taking a step backwards, away from her.

The shock of his rejection was so powerful, so painful, that Catherine actually had to press a frantic hand to her lips to hold back the cry of pain that almost escaped her. And, seeing it, Evan let his mouth curve into a cruel travesty of a smile.

'You see, Cat, there's one thing you should remember about the sick bastard that's stalking you, and that is that the guy's sexually obsessed with you. He would never be able to do this...'

Gently, but irresistibly, he drew that betraying hand from her mouth, and once more she felt the warmth of his kiss on her lips, heartbreakingly meaningless and agonisingly brief before he lifted his head again, looking deep into her shadowed eyes.

'And walk away. But I can...'

And, deliberately turning his back on her, he walked out of the room without even a glance at her face, letting the door slam behind him with a bang that shattered what was left of her self-control.

With hot tears burning in her eyes, Catherine could only think of one thing—to escape to the sanctuary of her room and there lick her wounds in peace. But the real trouble was that even as she reached the stairs and began to stumble blindly up them she knew she wasn't just running from Evan but from her own whirling thoughts, the burning images etched into her mind.

She was trying to escape from the primitive, yearning ache of desire that even so cold and calculated a kiss could awaken in her. But deep in her heart she knew that no matter how far or how fast she ran she could never escape from herself.

CHAPTER NINE

IF CIRCUMSTANCES had been different, then the last few days could have been absolute bliss, Catherine thought to herself, stretching luxuriously in the heat of the sun as she lay on a red and white striped sun-lounger beside the farm's swimming pool.

It seemed like an age since she had felt so relaxed, so free from tension. For the past six months the pressure had been so intense, so unremitting, that it was only now, when she had been released from it, that she really realised just how bad it had been. She couldn't believe how good it felt no longer to fear the telephone, the arrival of the post, not to worry that someone might be spying on her. The sense of release was so wonderful it was intoxicating, making her feel on a permanent high.

And the weather had been so glorious too—hot, sunny days, without a cloud in the sky. It was like being on holiday.

'I think you've been out here quite long enough.'

The cool, clipped voice broke into her reverie, making her start nervously, all her former sense of relaxation evaporating swiftly as she glanced up sharply.

'You'll burn if you stay any longer.'

Catherine scowled up at the tall figure of the one thing that stopped her pleasure from being complete. Evan Lindsay, the proverbial fly in the ointment—and a very big fly indeed, both physically and emotionally.

'I'm not stupid!' She picked up her watch from where it lay beside her and consulted it ostentatiously. 'There's another ten minutes before I need to think of covering up.'

If it hadn't been for the fact that it would have made him think he had won, she might have given in to the temptation to reach for her wrap. The simple black bikini she wore was modest by Mediterranean beach standards, but with Evan towering over her in this way, and those cool aquamarine eyes regarding her with such a lack of emotion—lack of anything—she felt decidedly uncomfortable.

'I do know about safe sunbathing.'

'And safe sex?' he shot back. 'Do you practise that too? Oh, I'm not talking about protecting yourself from pregnancy or AIDS,' he went on as Catherine's mouth fell open in shocked indignation, 'from what I've seen of you, you don't strike me as being so much of a fool as to ignore *that*—'

'How very gracious of you!'

'But what about the risks involved in choosing the wrong sort of partner? Someone—'

'Are you still harping on about the fact that Joe might be an ex-lover of mine? Because if so spare yourself the trouble! I've thought it over again and again, and there's no way it could be anyone like that. Besides, there just isn't—'

'Isn't what?' Evan pounced when she broke off in consternation at what she had been about to reveal.

'If you must know, there aren't any candidates!' Provoked beyond endurance, she flung the words at him. 'For one thing I've never had the scores of lovers you seem to expect, and Will . . .'

Her expression softened abruptly, her mouth curving into a gentle smile.

'Will would never do anything like this.'

'How can you be so sure?'

'I know him! He's sweet and gentle and—'

Seeing Evan's stony expression, she sighed.

'All right, if you want chapter and verse. One—'

Unconsciously she mirrored Evan's own technique of elucidating the points of evidence, counting them on her fingers as he had done that first night.

'We were very good friends when we parted, and we've stayed that way. Two—he's married, and three—he now lives in Tasmania.'

The tiny flare of triumph she felt at scoring even this minor point faded rapidly when Evan said, 'And this Will—was he the only one?'

Did he want blood?

'Yes!' She hissed through clenched teeth, fighting an urge to reach for the wrap she had scorned earlier and cover herself, hiding the raised colour of her skin from his eyes.

'Why so worried, Cat?' Evan asked softly. 'Do you really believe I'll think less of you because you're not the sort of so-called liberated woman who changes lovers as often as she does her clothes? If so, you couldn't be more wrong.'

'Will was the proverbial boy next door.' Something about the conviction that rang in his voice, the unexpected warmth in his eyes, drew the words from her. 'We sort of grew up together—went to the same school, the same parties. We even went on to the same university, where we were both so scared we clung together for comfort. In a way, our affair was just a boy-girl thing.'

'It certainly sounds very innocent—and, yes, I agree, he hardly sounds like a potential candidate for the role of Joe. I just thought that perhaps somewhere, some time, you'd met a man who might have felt more for you than you did for him—or, rather, who thought he did. Because these types don't really *care* for the object of their attentions, they just want power over them— they want to possess them...'

For a moment his words faded as from the back of her mind came a faint echo of a memory, something called up by what he had said, but as she strained to remember more clearly it slid away, leaving her with the cold, creeping sensation of someone having walked over her grave.

'Are you cold?' Evan had caught her involuntary shiver.

'No...'

But nevertheless unease had her sitting up, reaching for her wrap and pushing her arms into the sleeves with disturbed haste.

'It was just what you said about wanting power—it made me remember why we're here, what I've escaped from.'

'Cat—' Evan came down onto the seat next to her, taking her hands in his as he had on that first day. '—you're quite safe here.'

'I know—but how long can I stay here? I mean, it's been a week already.'

'You know you can stay as long as you like.'

'But I can't stay *for ever*. One day I'll have to go back—if only because, inevitably, at some point my two months' leave will run out. And what if the police haven't found him?'

'I'll still be there. I promised you—I'm not leaving you alone until you know just who he is.'

When he had looked into her eyes like that on that first night, holding her hands in just this way, she had felt that she could trust him with her life, that she could put herself into those hands with total confidence. And, in a way inspired by that one irrational leap of faith, she had done just that. She had been so very sure then—so why couldn't she feel the same way now?

Because she was no longer quite so naïve. She had seen other, less flattering sides of Evan Lindsay—the cold calculation, the ruthless, domineering force—and, as he had so deliberately set out to prove to her, she knew that until Joe was caught she couldn't really trust anyone.

'That's a promise, Cat.'

'I know.'

And he always kept his promises. It should reassure her, so why didn't it?

Because there was more to it than just not trusting anyone. On that first evening Evan had just been someone who knew about security—a potential body-guard—someone who could be at her side when her father was on the other side of the world. Now the re-lationship between them had changed—slowly and subtly, as a landscape changed through the day as the sun moved from east to west, highlighting different areas, shadowing others. It was the same and yet no longer as she had first seen it.

Evan was no longer just someone who could provide the protection she needed. Over the past days her awareness of him as a man had been growing steadily and disturbingly. From the start there had been that magnetic pull, the way her skin tingled, the way her heart leapt into an accelerated beat when he walked into the room, and now just the touch of his hand on hers made her whole body sing in response, her breathing quick-ening so that it was almost impossible to think.

'I know,' she managed again, with a tenuous smile. 'And—thanks.'

'No problem.'

With a jarring abruptness, her hands were dropped into her lap. He had achieved the result he had aimed for, making her relax as he had wanted.

'And now, what about a day out? You must be bored rigid, stuck here like this.'

'I'm fine...'

She bent her head to fasten the ties on her wrap, in order to conceal her face as she spoke, hide the disap-pointment that must darken her eyes. Because Evan felt nothing of the way she did; that much was painfully clear. Even when she had been wearing just the black bikini he hadn't looked anywhere but straight into her eyes, his only indication of the fact that he was aware of her undressed state being the comment about making sure she didn't burn. And, in spite of everything she did to try and stop it, that cool indifference stung bitterly.

'But wouldn't you like a day out? I could do with going into Lincoln—you'd be perfectly safe,' he added, seeing her worried look.

That wasn't what was troubling her. At the moment she was more concerned with the thought of spending a day with him in her present state of heightened awareness.

'Are you sure you could spare the time from your precious horses?'

One of the things she had discovered when she had finally emerged from her self-imposed isolation in her bedroom was the fact that, contrary to her belief that the farm was just a country hideaway, it was in fact a working concern, devoted to the breeding of horses. Evan had shown her round, taking her down to the fields where she had been unable to contain her delight at the sight of the gentle mares and their big-eyed, long-legged foals, some of them only weeks old.

'The farm can take care of itself for a while. After all, I do have an excellent manager, who is paid very highly to run things when I'm not here. Come on, Cat, say yes! We could have dinner somewhere too—I know some excellent restaurants.'

When he smiled like that, his voice softening cajolingly, it was impossible to resist him—and why should she? If she was honest, the prospect of an afternoon in Lincoln—a city she had never visited—was very appealing.

'All right,' she said, and was rewarded by a devastating increase in the brilliance of that smile, turning it to a megawatt brilliance that made her mind reel under its impact.

'Great! Why don't you go inside and make yourself presentable while I change, and we can meet at the car in say, twenty minutes?'

'Make yourself presentable', Catherine repeated to herself, with a touch of resentment as she surveyed herself in the bathroom mirror a few minutes later. She would hardly have described herself as *un*presentable!

It was true that her hair was a little windblown and tangled after her swim, and that her nose was touched with pink after lying in the sun, but that didn't make her unattractive! On the contrary, she personally felt that the wash of colour in her cheeks put some life into a face that for too long had been pallid and drained by stress.

But perhaps Evan's preference was for the smoothly sophisticated type. Perhaps he liked his women cool and elegant—that might account for his apparent indifference to her.

Suddenly, a rush of purely feminine pique surged through her, firing her resolve and making her blue eyes gleam determinedly.

Indifferent, was he? Well, she'd show him! Moving with a new sense of purpose, she stripped off the black bikini and stepped into the shower.

Twenty minutes later she was heading downstairs again, totally transformed from the windblown creature who had been by the pool. Her fair hair, subtly highlighted by a week in the sun, hung in a sleek, gleaming mane down to her shoulders, curling under smoothly at the ends. Her face was perfectly but delicately made up, with just a touch of colour on her cheekbones to emphasise the soft tan she was developing, her wide-spaced eyes enhanced by smoky taupe shadow and several coats of mascara and her lips by a sheer rose lipstick.

She wore a soft blue sleeveless linen dress, V-necked and buttoning all the way down the front, that picked up and deepened the shade of her eyes. She'd added a white cotton jacket against the cool of the evening, and, as her legs were brown enough to dispense with tights, she had slipped delicate, high-heeled bronze leather sandals onto her bare feet.

She didn't know what had possessed her to pack those particular shoes when she had chosen her selection of clothes in her flat, but privately admitted that perhaps she had been subject to a subconscious longing for just such an occasion as this.

'Well?' she demanded as soon as she saw Evan standing in the hallway. 'What do you think?'

She twirled round before him, sending her hair and the softly flaring dress spinning in a circle, her perfume wafting towards him on the air as she smiled straight into his eyes.

'More *presentable*?' Her tone was deliberately flirtatious.

She didn't know quite what reaction she'd anticipated; certainly not the one she got. Evan's response was almost insulting in its blandness. Turning a swift, appraising glance on her, he simply nodded.

'Very smart,' he murmured. 'Right, let's go.'

'Smart'? Catherine thought furiously. 'Very *smart*'! Surely even he could do better than that! Without vanity, she knew that she looked good, and her smouldering resentment wasn't helped by the fact that Evan himself looked good enough to eat.

There should be a law against his sort of appeal, she reflected edgily as she followed him out to the car. The loose, oatmeal-coloured summer-weight suit and the pale green polo shirt he wore underneath it enhanced the colour of his eyes, making them glow like cut emeralds in the sunlight.

With the sun on his hair, burnishing it to the sheen of highly polished wood, and the tan that he seemed to have acquired effortlessly after the days spent around the farm touching his skin with gold, he was altogether too perfect a specimen of masculinity for her to feel comfortable at the prospect of sitting close to him in the confined space of the car for any length of time.

She couldn't be unaware of the way that the supremely civilised clothing emphasised rather than subdued the almost primitive forcefulness of his male strength—the softness of the material contrasting sharply with the hard power of the honed muscles beneath.

'Will it take us long to get to Lincoln?' She had to talk, to say something innocuous, if only to distract herself from the way she was feeling.

Evan shook his head, making one dark lock fall forward over his brow, and Catherine's fingers itched to be able to smooth it back.

'Just under an hour if we go along Ermine Street— that's the old Roman road, so it's practically in a straight line.'

'Tell me something—why is the farm called such an unusual name? I would have thought that Dragon Farm would have been more appropriate in Wales.'

Evan's grin did uncomfortable things to her insides, making her clench her hands in her lap under the concealing drape of her cotton jacket.

'Would you believe that there's supposed to be a dragon buried in a village just a couple of miles from here? I'm not sure whether it's dead or just sleeping, but it's said that that's how Dragonby got its name.'

'Dragons and the Romans? It doesn't quite go together.'

'The Vikings were here too—by and thorpe are Viking words—and they had dragon ships.'

'Of course. I forgot that we're not all that far from the coast. Why did you decide to move here?'

'Oh, I didn't decide,' Evan astounded her by saying. 'This is home to me. I was born in this part of the country—well, Nottingham, actually, but that's only a few miles away. And I spent all my childhood holidays with my maternal grandparents near Mablethorpe, where they had a small hotel. So when I was looking for somewhere to start the stud naturally I looked for a place around here.'

'And did you always have an interest in horses? Like Romans and dragons, it doesn't seem to combine with security.'

Something changed in Evan's face, his long body suddenly taut in a way that it hadn't been before.

'No. A long time ago, I vowed I'd have nothing to do with breeding or anything like it—even though I grew up with horses. My father trains racehorses—he has stables up at Malton. We—didn't get on when I was in my teens, and I was determined I'd do something very different from his way of life.'

'You said that was why you joined the army.'

'Yeah.' Evan's tone was wry. 'I signed up as an act of rebellion—asserting my independence—and regretted it from day one. But I was too proud or too damn stubborn to admit it. So I stayed put and learned a lot, but when I came out I knew that that sort of lifestyle was definitely not for me. So I went to university and studied business and marketing, and when I left there I applied it to the practical knowledge I'd learned.'

'Security?'

Evan nodded. 'And things grew from there.'

'What about the problem with your father?' Catherine asked the question tentatively, not sure whether he would consider that she was trespassing, venturing into territory he preferred to keep private.

But Evan answered easily enough.

'Much the same as yours with your mother. A broken marriage—only in my case it was my father who was in the wrong. I found out that he'd met another woman when I was fifteen, and I just couldn't accept it. I wouldn't forgive him for being unfaithful to my mother, even though she later admitted that their relationship had been dead for years.'

Catherine could just imagine him then—young, idealistic, and desperately loyal to his mother, his adolescent temper on a hairspring trigger. The image tugged at her heart.

'Is there still a problem?'

Evan paused at a junction, negotiating the awkward turn before replying.

'No. I grew up—calmed down and started listening—and he stopped shouting and started talking. It helped that I liked his new wife—and when my sister was born that finally sorted everything out.'

Something shivered over Catherine's nerves in response to the softening of his voice. Obviously his half-sister meant a great deal to him.

'But I thought—when you said you met my mother—'

'At Sam's party? Oh, he's married to Emma. She's my big sister—rapidly approaching the big four-oh and dreading the prospect. Beth's the baby of the family.'

And she had him wrapped tightly around her little finger, putty in her hands; it was obvious.

'I envy you your family,' she said softly.

'We have our ups and downs, but generally we're a source of support and strength for each other.' Evan shot her one of those swift, sidelong glances. 'Forgive your mother, Cat,' he said, startling her with the accuracy with which he had read her thoughts. 'You'll only hurt yourself if you don't.'

'I think I already have,' Catherine sighed. 'After all, I hardly knew her. It's just for Dad that I still feel so bad about it all. She was the love of his life, and as I said, he's never really looked at another woman since.'

'Some people are like that.' There was a strange note in Evan's voice, one she couldn't even begin to interpret. 'They meet someone and lose their heart in the blink of an eyelid, and no matter what happens later they can't do a thing about it.'

Had that happened to him? Catherine couldn't help wondering. But she knew it was too intimate a question to ask. The effect on her own mental equilibrium of just the thought of that was devastating, and she had to clench her hands tightly, digging her nails into her palms, using the small physical pain to distract herself from the emotional whirlwind inside her head.

'But just because your father's never recovered from the way your mother behaved that doesn't mean you should let it blight your life too. You can't hide or erase the characteristics that you've inherited from Melissa—they're part of you, too, even if you felt you had to leave home before you could express them fully.'

He'd done it again, Catherine thought on a wave of shock. He'd probed deep into the secret parts of her heart and seen things that she rarely talked to anyone about.

'Dad always said that he couldn't stand my clutter, but I knew it was because it reminded him of the way my mother was. When she left he had all her decorations and colour schemes ripped out and eradicated, and redid things in the very simple, elegant way he said he preferred. It's been like that ever since, but I've seen photographs of how it used to be, and I loved them.

'And then, when I wanted to work in the media, I was afraid he'd see it as a betrayal—that I was following in her footsteps. I think he was scared it would take me away from him.'

'It would never do that. And you can only ever be yourself, Cat.'

They had reached the outskirts of the city now, and Evan had to concentrate on the road, but his tone was gentle and warm.

'You've got bits of both your father and mother in you, but you're not either of them—you're yourself, and that self is very special—unique.'

'I just hope I haven't inherited my mother's inability to make a lasting relationship.'

She didn't know why she'd said that. She'd never admitted it to another living soul. Perhaps it had something to do with trying to ignore the effect his words and the tone in which they'd been spoken had had on her. Suddenly she felt as if all the feelings she had experienced in the course of the journey had tied themselves in a tight knot in her throat, and that she could hardly breathe.

'Is that what's worrying you? Well, I shouldn't let it, because from what I've seen I don't think that would be your problem at all. Here we are...'

'Already?'

Catherine couldn't believe that the journey had passed so quickly. She had been so caught up in their conversation she had barely noticed her surroundings.

'Is that the cathedral?'

'That's right—and behind this high wall on our right is the castle. That—' he pointed to a cobbled street that seemed to drop away almost vertically '—is the aptly named Steep Hill, which leads down to the centre—and partway down it is one of my very favourite places to eat. So now—' that smile was turned on her in full force '—all you have to decide is where you'd like to start.'

What she really wanted to start with was finding out just what he had meant by that last cryptic remark, but from Evan's tone and demeanour it was evident that the time for questions was past. She would come back to it later, she promised herself, consulting her watch.

'Well, it's barely twelve so we could fit in some history before we eat. How about exploring the castle?'

Laughter bubbled up inside her at his assumption of an expression of deep disappointment.

'I shall fade away with hunger,' he grumbled, but he was smiling. 'All right—the castle it is.'

CHAPTER TEN

'I'M EXHAUSTED!'

Catherine slumped down on the settee and kicked off her shoes with a sigh of relief, stretching her slim legs out in front of her.

'But it was a wonderful day—dinner was fabulous. Thank you so much!'

'My pleasure,' Evan returned easily. 'But it doesn't have to end yet.'

'No?'

Intrigued, Catherine turned to him. He had been the perfect escort all day, polite, attentive—and he hadn't even complained when she had insisted on investigating a wonderful little dress shop.

But then, she added to herself ruefully, neither had he shown any more than an objective interest in the dresses she had tried on, even though, driven by some imp of mischief, she had chosen the most flattering and—with the heat of the day a perfect excuse—the most revealing outfits she could find to wear as she paraded up and down in front of him.

He had simply observed her performance with grave interest, saying only that they all looked good on her—'attractive' was the most emotive word he had used—until she had been ready to scream with frustration. What did she have to do to get this man to notice she was a woman?

'It's still fairly early. Perhaps you'd like a nightcap—or would you prefer to get straight to bed?'

'What?'

With her thoughts still on her attempt to provoke some reaction from him—any reaction—Catherine stared at him in blank confusion, her blue eyes wide and shocked. But then sanity reasserted itself in the moment that Evan laughed.

'Oh, Cat, you surely didn't think I was propositioning you—did you? It's just that every night this week you've rushed off to bed as soon as the clock's struck ten, like some modern-day Cinderella who knows she'll turn into a pumpkin if she stays around any longer.'

'I "rushed off to bed" as you put it, because I was tired.'

She prayed that the firmness of her tone would draw his attention away from the tide of colour that she could feel rising in her cheeks.

'I haven't slept at all well for weeks, but here I've been able to relax, so that it's all caught up with me.'

Her explanation seemed to satisfy him, she saw with relief, knowing that if he had probed any further she would have been hard put to it to hide the fact that her own ambiguous feelings about him had been more responsible for her early nights than any real tiredness. After all, when she had got to bed she had rarely slept until long after Evan himself had come upstairs, kept awake by restless thoughts that went round and round in unproductive circles in her head.

As for the dreams she experienced once she had fallen asleep, she preferred to draw a veil over them! The fact that they were filled with images of Evan, images that were coloured with a dark, burning sensuality that she hadn't known herself capable of feeling, was something she didn't admit to willingly—even to herself.

'But tonight I feel much better, so—yes—a nightcap would be lovely.'

If ever there was a time to make him admit that he wasn't indifferent to her, then surely this was it, she thought, curling her legs up underneath her on the huge, bronze velvet-covered settee. After a day spent in the sun, and a candlelit dinner, if they talked late into the night...

'I thought perhaps we could listen to some music,' Evan suggested, and Catherine was swift to smile her agreement. Soft music, dim lights—it got better and better. 'It would be the perfect opportunity to show you that all opera doesn't sound like some poor cat being tortured.'

The smile slipped slightly, but she dragged it back into place.

'OK, I'm game. What did you have in mind?'

'Mozart—*The Marriage of Figaro*—or perhaps Strauss?'

'Mozart, please. At least I know I like some of his stuff—*Eine kleine Nachtmusik* and all that. You know,' she added worriedly as Evan selected a CD and put it on, 'I'm not at all sure I'm going to enjoy this. I'm really a musical ignoramus.'

'You don't have to know anything in order to enjoy it,' Evan laughed, coming to sit on the chair opposite. 'Just lie back and relax,' he went on as the first strains of music crept into the room. 'Let it wash over you.'

Relax! Catherine thought dazedly. When he looked at her like that, and that rich, warm voice slid over her nerves with the ease of molten honey, it was all she could do not to melt into a liquid pool of pleasure right at his feet.

But she did as he said, and found it surprisingly easy to let herself drift, the beauty of the music taking over and drawing any last traces of tension from her. Suddenly she found herself totally caught up in the experience, the words—in translation—making sense at last as they blended perfectly with the music.

'I enjoyed that!' she said a long time later, as the final chords died away.

'I thought you might. Perhaps we'll try something else another time.'

'I'd like to. So now what—coffee?'

'Wouldn't that keep you awake?'

'I'm willing to risk it.' She wouldn't be able to sleep anyway, and she was willing to risk anything that would keep him with her like this, in this wonderfully relaxed, easy mood.

'OK, you put the kettle on.' Evan was on his feet and heading for the kitchen. 'There's something I have to do.'

'What?'

Catherine padded after him on bare feet, and was amazed to see him hunt in a cupboard, pulling out a tin and reaching for the can-opener.

'What's this? Cat food? But you don't have a cat.'

'No.' Evan's grin was boyish. 'But I do have a four-legged friend.'

'What—?' But he laid a finger over her mouth when she would have asked more.

'You make the coffee, then come into the dining-room and you'll see what I mean.'

A few minutes later, Catherine couldn't control her curiosity any longer as she placed the coffee-cups on the table. Evan was on the patio, visible through the open French windows.

'Just what's going on?'

'Shh...' He straightened from where he had been spooning the meat into a small dog's bowl and came inside to join her. 'Just be quiet and watch.'

He came to stand beside her, and she struggled to concentrate on the sense of anticipation, wondering just what was going to happen, in order to distract herself from the crazy, head-spinning sense of excitement his closeness brought, the singing awareness in every nerve, the shiver of friction as his arm brushed hers briefly.

'Listen...'

Ears straining, Catherine caught a faint snuffling sound, coming closer. Then as she watched a small creature appeared in the circle of light from the open doorway, dark brown and spiky, with bright eyes and a little black button nose.

'A hedgehog!' In her delight, it was difficult to control the level of her voice, but the little animal was too intent on the food to be distracted.

'That's the male—he always eats first,' Evan said softly as the hedgehog buried its nose in the bowl of cat food. 'When he's finished, his mate gets her share.'

'He's so cute!'

Catherine watched, transfixed, her smile a reflection of her pleasure as they stood in companionable silence. Even without a word being spoken, it was a moment of such pure, instinctive sharing that there was perfect communication between them, nothing needing to be said. But then Evan moved slightly, to sling an arm around her shoulders, and the feel of its warm, heavy weight was both a source of pleasure and an unnerving distraction, setting her heart pounding with such intensity that she was sure he must hear it in the silence of the night.

At last the hedgehog moved, scuttling away into the darkness with a surprising speed, his movements so comical that in spite of her disturbed state of mind she laughed out loud.

'I'm so glad I saw that. Thank you for sharing it with me.'

She twisted in his arms as she spoke, her face tilting up towards his, her eyes sparkling in the moonlight, her hair falling down her back in a pale waterfall, touched with silver. Evan's face was in darkness, his eyes just deep, shadowed pools, hidden and unreadable, but something about him, a difference she could sense intuitively, a new tension in the long body so close to hers, alerted her to his change of mood.

For a long, taut moment he stared down at her, his mouth tight, his eyes hooded, his expression giving nothing away, and Catherine felt her throat dry in nervousness, her tongue slipping out to moisten her lips, her heart giving a quiver of apprehension as she saw the way his gaze, silvered by the moon, dropped to follow the small, betraying movement.

Now! her mind cried. *Now*! Surely the perfect way to end this evening, with its peace, the happiness they had shared—the music, the final delight of the hedgehog's appearance—was to seal it all with a kiss. She was so sure that that was what Evan wanted too that she even lifted her face towards his, offering her lips.

'Well, I don't know about you, but I'm shattered.'

Evan's matter-of-fact tone slashed through her daydream like an icy blade, freezing her blood in her veins so that she could only blink in shock.

'Climbing Steep Hill in this heat just about finished me off.'

It was only when he moved out of her grasp that she realised the way her arms had been around his narrow waist, her hands linked in the small of his back, and now they fell to her sides with a jarring abruptness. Too numb, too emotionally bruised to speak, she could only watch in silence as Evan shut and locked the windows, jerking the curtains over them with an abruptness that seemed to communicate his rejection of her more clearly than any words he might speak.

'Goodnight, Cat. Sleep well.'

And then he did kiss her, but the brief, sharp peck on her cheek could never have been described as sensual or even faintly amorous. It was barely even brotherly.

'Sleep well'! The words echoed in Catherine's head as she watched him go, taking the stairs two at a time in a way that, even if she hadn't already been sure, would have revealed his tiredness for the fiction it was. There was little chance of her sleeping at all, feeling the way she did. Her whole body was taut as a violin string, wide awake and yearning for the very thing that had been snatched away from it so abruptly.

The feeling was so bitter, so painful, that when she turned and saw Evan's coffee-mug, untouched and still steaming slightly on the table where she had placed it, mute evidence of the way he had rejected her—because he must have known how she'd felt—it was all she could do not to snatch it up and fling it into the fireplace, watching it shatter into pieces like her own private hopes.

Considering her mood when she went to bed, and the hot, humid atmosphere of the night, it was probably inevitable that when Catherine finally fell into an uneasy doze her sleep was plagued by dreams so vivid and darkly disturbing that they had her tossing and turning in her bed.

She was being pursued, chased by a shrouded, faceless figure. Joe had tracked her down, and now he had finally caught up with her. She tried to run from him, but it felt as if her feet were covered in thick, sticky tar so that she couldn't lift them from the road. Desperately afraid, she looked back over her shoulder, only to find that the creature behind her was gaining ground, coming closer—closer... And now she could see his face, see the cold aquamarine eyes. *Evan's* eyes—Evan's face.

'Oh, no! No! *No!*'

'Catherine? Cat? You're dreaming—wake up.'

At first she thought that the voice was part of her dream, a dreadful confirmation of her fears, but then warm hands lifted her from her pillows, strong arms gathering her close, and as her eyelids fluttered she realised that the solidity and hard strength she rested against was Evan's chest—Evan's *naked* chest—his skin warm and smooth under her cheek. The realisation of that fact was so disturbing that her eyes flew open swiftly, to stare straight into Evan's watchful face.

'Oh!' It was a sobbing gasp, with the image of her dream, of that terrifying face still there in her mind. 'Oh, *Evan!*'

'Joe?'

Intuitively he knew what had troubled her—*part* of what had troubled her—and as she nodded miserably she wished it were just that simple. Evan swore violently, and his arms tightened round her.

'You've nothing to fear, Cat. I'll not let him harm you. I told you, I'll keep you safe.'

It was weak, it was foolish, in fact it was downright stupid, but when he held her like this she didn't *care*— about anything. Joe could come—a dozen Joes, all armed to the teeth—and it wouldn't worry her. All she wanted was to stay like this, in the stronghold of Evan's arms, with the warm silk of his skin under her cheek, the dark hair that shaded it rough against her skin, the heavy thud of his heart in her ear.

And it was that heartbeat that gave him away. Because as she stirred, coming fully awake at last, the steady rhythm altered, changing to a heavier, less even pattern, and in the same second that she registered the significance of this reaction her sensitive hearing caught his swiftly indrawn breath.

'Evan...'

There was no thought now of proving herself attractive, of deliberately rousing his interest. She was beyond such feelings, and besides, there was no need. The man who held her, whose powerful body was taut with a hungry tension that matched her own, was as aware of her as she was of him. Instantly all the overwhelming feelings that had been awoken in her earlier that night, only to be ruthlessly squashed down again, rushed to the surface of her mind, making her head swim with the force of their impact.

Evan—kiss me!

She didn't actually say the words—her heart was beating too high up in her throat for her to have been able to get them out without choking—but she knew that they must be clear in her eyes—as plain to see as if they were etched in fiery letters ten feet tall.

Kiss me!

And at last Evan's mouth came down on hers, and this time it was no tiny peck, or anything that could have been remotely described as brotherly. Instead it was a kiss that was raw with passion and need—a need that mirrored her own so perfectly that she surrendered mindlessly, unhesitatingly, any doubts, any fears swept away under the force of the burning torrent of feeling that raged through her.

And then she was kissing him back, taking his mouth with desperate, greedy hunger. Her hands seemed to have developed a life of their own as they smoothed and caressed the satin skin of his back, feeling the powerful muscles bunch underneath her fingertips. She laughed in triumph as he shivered in response to the light scratch of her nails all the way down his spine.

Evan's hands were not idle either, his touch burning erotic patterns over her skin, dispensing easily with the shoestring straps of the white nightdress, finding the yearning sensitivity of her breasts, closing over them with a controlled force that made her cry her delight out loud.

That cry was choked off in her throat as Evan replaced the warmth of his fingers with the more forceful heat of his mouth, the pleasure he woke in her too great to be communicated in any way but by the silence of total concentration.

For long, ecstatic seconds she lay frozen, every part of her being centred on the tiny pleasure-point, the heat that radiated out from it flooding her whole body. She never wanted him to stop, and yet she felt that it was too much—any more and she would die.

But then at last he released her, his lips, softer now, trailing burning kisses up towards the arched column of her throat.

'Evan!'

His name was a sigh of joy before his mouth closed over hers again, kissing her even more fiercely this time, urgent and demanding—and yet...

Suddenly, at some deep, intuitive level, she knew that something had changed. He wasn't with her any more—not in the same way. Somehow, at some point she had lost him. The tiny seed of doubt had barely had time to take root in her thoughts before her fear was confirmed by the way that Evan suddenly pulled himself away from her, stilling her protests with his fingers across her lips.

'That's enough,' he said, and his very calmness, the icy determination that gleamed in his eyes, stilled her more effectively than his words.

This was not a decision she could fight; she knew that instinctively. And if she had needed any confirmation of that fact, he gave it to her in the way he pulled the front of her nightdress back up across her aching breasts, moving the straps into place on her shoulders, his actions, his touch as cool and clinical as the unyielding expression in his face. He had meant what he had said—and yet she had to try.

Heedless of the possible consequences, she pulled away from his restraining hand.

'Evan—please—' she began, but he shook his head in deliberate rejection of anything she might say, already off the bed and several steps away from her—mentally as well as physically.

'*Enough*, Cat,' he repeated obdurately. 'Now isn't the time. We'll talk about this in the morning. Sleep now—and no more dreams.'

And then he was gone, leaving her burning up with frustration, her mind just a raw, agonising wound. How could he have stopped like that? How could he have pulled back so coolly and calmly when she couldn't have denied him anything? He must have known that—even now her body still throbbed in the aftermath of his lovemaking.

Or what she had believed was lovemaking. *Could* Evan be indifferent to her after all? Was it possible?

No! Every feminine instinct she possessed screamed that that thought was crazy. Evan had been every bit as aroused as she was. So had his ruthless imposition of a control she'd neither wanted nor welcomed been a form of consideration—a concern for her, an unexpected unwillingness to let her rush into something she might regret later? If so, it turned on its head the accusation she had flung at him on the first morning at the farm, making her declaration that he could be the stalker into so much nonsense.

Would Joe, a man who in Evan's own words was sexually obsessed, be capable of such an action?

Unless, of course, that withdrawal and the apparent consideration he had shown were actions as calculated and coldly thought out as the first time he had made love to her. Then he had been able to turn a sexual response on and off at will, making her believe he was aroused and then making it painfully plain that he was not. So did he now want her to believe that, unlike Joe, he could be restrained and thoughtful where she was concerned? And if so, why?

And out of all these possibilities which persona revealed the true Evan? And—perhaps more important—which one did she *want* him to be?

Dear God, she didn't know what to think!

CHAPTER ELEVEN

THE first thing Catherine noticed when, bleary-eyed from lack of sleep, she finally made her way downstairs was the coat—a lightweight cotton jacket in the sort of bright pink that she knew she would have remembered if she had ever seen it before—hanging on the wooden coatstand at the far end of the hall.

Then as she paused, staring at it in confusion, she heard voices—Evan's deep tones, sounding disturbingly warm and affectionate, and mixed in with them the lighter, laughing sound of a woman. A woman she didn't know. Her confusion growing, she flung open the kitchen door to find Evan seated at the scrubbed pine table, a mug of coffee in his hand, and sitting opposite him a pretty, dark-haired girl whose green eyes sparkled with amusement at something he had just said.

'Oh—hi!'

Before she had time to do more than register the scene before her, note the slightly speculative look in Evan's eyes as they went to her face, the unknown girl had flashed her a wide, brilliant smile.

'You must be Catherine. I hope you don't mind, but I just had to meet you. You see, I just love your show— oh, I know that at sixteen I'm supposed to be too old for it, but I watch it with Emma's brood, and we all think it's great. So when Ev here phoned and told me that you were here I just had to come and see what you were really like.'

Ev, Catherine noted with a touch of amazement. She couldn't imagine Evan letting many people get away with that! Clearly this girl was special.

'Brat, be quiet!' Evan put in reprovingly. 'Catherine's only just got up, and she's very fragile in the mornings. In case you hadn't guessed, Cat, this is my kid sister, Beth—she's staying with our grandparents.'

But Catherine had finally registered precisely what Beth had said.

'When he *phoned*! So it's one law for you and another for everyone else, is it?' she demanded furiously, and Evan at least had the grace to look slightly shamefaced.

'Oh, I don't count,' Beth put in, blithely oblivious to the undercurrents swirling around the other two people in the room. 'I'm family. You can trust me not to tell anyone—not even Ma and Pa—though I'm sure even Dad has realised by now that at your advanced age you're old enough to have ladyfriends staying over, brother dear.' She directed a wicked teasing smile at the man opposite.

So Evan hadn't told Beth the real reason why she was here, Catherine realised, which of course meant that his sister had put two and two together and come up with five.

'That's enough, horror! Catherine—would you like breakfast?'

'Just coffee, thanks.'

Catherine couldn't decide whether to see Beth's unexpected visit as a relief or an intrusion. At least her presence in the room acted as a welcome buffer against the awkwardness of being with Evan after the events of the previous night—but equally it meant that there was no possibility of discussing those events with him until she had gone.

'I don't know how you can drink coffee in this heat!' Beth exclaimed, fanning herself with her hand. 'I'm boiled!'

'You're not wearing enough to be boiled,' Evan told her, with a nod towards the shoestring straps and very mini skirt of the red and white slip of a dress his sister wore. 'That thing is barely decent.'

'And I suppose your Catherine's outfit is *so* much more modest?'

Thanks, Beth, Catherine thought ironically as the younger girl's words brought those sea-coloured eyes swinging round to her once more, the look in them making her want to reach for a teatowel or something similar, and hold it up in front of her as a form of protection.

In her room that morning, she had mentally tossed a coin in order to decide what to wear—not knowing whether to go with her inclination to choose something that was all-concealing, covering her from top to toe, in the hope of erasing all memory of the previous night in order to avoid any possible repetition of those events, or to continue with her plan to prove Evan's declaration that he was indifferent to her as the lie it was.

In the end, the heat of the sun already streaming through the window had pushed her into a decision, but not before she had admitted to herself that having come this far she could not go back—and if she was honest she didn't want to. Whatever was going to happen, she wanted it out in the open now.

And so she had chosen clothes that reflected her mood. The sleeveless, self-embroidered white shirt was of such fine cotton that it was almost see-through, and she had knotted it tightly under her breasts, exposing inches of lightly tanned midriff. With it, she had on a pair of sunshine-yellow shorts that flattered the golden slenderness of her legs, making them look longer than ever.

In the privacy of her bedroom the outfit had looked youthfully light-hearted, a bit flirtatious, but now, seeing the way Evan's eyes had narrowed, their sudden darkness, she felt her confidence seeping away, seeing it instead as provocative in the extreme.

'I—was planning a morning by the pool,' she said hurriedly, knowing from his expression that the explanation hadn't convinced him.

'Great idea! I'll join you.' Beth bounced up from her chair. 'Ev has business calls to make, so we can have some girly time together—and perhaps a swim later on.'

Not on your life, Catherine thought privately, forcing a smile. After the look Evan had just given her it took all her mental strength not to turn and dash upstairs and pull on jeans and a long-sleeved shirt, never mind stripping down to the revealing bikini she had sported so carelessly the day before.

Luckily for her peace of mind, those business calls occupied Evan for the rest of the morning, and he didn't join them until they all gathered in the kitchen once more to share a late lunch. Even then he seemed abstracted and distant, and it was only Beth's bright chatter that kept the meal from being an uncomfortably silent one. When they had all finished, Beth pushed back her chair and stood up.

'Oh, well, I'll have to be going. I promised Nan and Grandad I'd catch the three o'clock bus back, and it's after two now. Are you going to give me a lift into town, Ev darling?'

'Call yourself a taxi,' Evan returned hardly. 'I'll pay for it.'

'Why don't you take her back?' Catherine put in. 'Surely it won't take more than an hour or so.'

'You know why.'

Oh, yes, she knew—but she also knew that right now the prospect of a little time on her own was very appealing. She had always been someone who valued her privacy, and she and Evan had been living in each other's pockets for nearly two weeks now. Even happily married couples didn't spend that much time together.

'Look, there hasn't been any trouble for days. We haven't had any phone calls—'

Recalling the fact that Beth was unaware of the real reason for her presence at the farm, she cut herself off there, knowing that Evan could be in no doubt what she meant.

'It would be all right.'

'I don't think so—unless, of course, you came with us.'

But that was not what Catherine had in mind at all, and she shook her fair head firmly.

'No, I want to rest this afternoon. I'm worn out—I didn't get much sleep last night.'

If Evan felt the sting of the deliberately pointed remark, then he didn't show it.

'Oh, *please*, Evan,' Beth begged, turning her big green eyes on his stony face.

Putty in her hands, Catherine had thought when he had first talked of his sister, and now he proved her right as his expression softened reluctantly.

'Oh, all right,' he said, obviously unable to resist her pleading. 'If you're quite sure...'

'I'll be fine,' Catherine assured him. Joe didn't even know where they were. 'I'm just going to go to my room, lock the door, draw the curtains and crash out.'

Evan could not have been unaware of the double significance of that, her words emphasising the fact that she would take precautions to keep herself safe and that even if he stayed she did not plan to be available to talk about last night.

At last Evan was persuaded, and got to his feet.

'I'll get the car,' he told his sister. 'You get your jacket and be outside in five minutes flat.'

'He doesn't want to leave you,' Beth pronounced smugly as soon as he was out of earshot. 'Not that I blame him. I mean, he's obviously got it bad—has had for ages.'

'Pardon?' Catherine couldn't believe her ears. 'Are you saying—?'

'Oh, hasn't he told you?' Beth's grin was wide, disturbingly like her brother's. 'No, I suppose, knowing Ev, he wouldn't let on until he was absolutely sure of you. But between you and me, he's had the hots for you for ages—has done ever since last November, when we were all at Em's and he first saw you on the television...'

The sound of the telephone shrilling through the house jolted Catherine awake with a jarring suddenness, and she was off the settee and halfway out into the hall before her eyes had even opened. In spite of the story she had given Evan she hadn't actually intended to go to sleep, but had planned to use the time alone to do some much needed thinking. But her disturbed night had caught up with her before she knew what was happening.

Who could this be? Someone wanting Evan—or possibly Evan himself? Perhaps he had got held up— some problem with the car. At least at Dragon Farm she could answer the phone without fear.

'Hello, Honey.' That hateful, distorted voice, sounding even worse for having been unheard for so long, whispered in her ear, making her freeze in shock, all the old terror flooding back. 'You abandoned me, you bitch—'

'No— I—'

'Oh, yes, you did, Honey.'

Perhaps it was because she was no longer so used to hearing it, and perhaps distance had given her a little objectivity, but just for a second the detested voice sounded almost familiar—but when she tried to think about it the connection eluded her.

'You ran off—but it isn't going to work. You see, I know where you are. I know, and I'm coming—'

'No!'

In a panic she slammed the receiver down to cut him off, then immediately lifted it again, dropping it down onto the huge pine chest. At least that way he couldn't ring again. But she couldn't make herself move away, standing frozen to the spot with the disconnected burr echoing in her ears.

'I know where you are... and I'm coming—'

If only Evan would come back—she would feel safe again with him in the house. Oh, *why* had he had to go out, just at this point? It was such an appalling coincidence that just when he left the house for the very first time—

Or was it such a coincidence after all?

The sudden thought hit her with such force that she reeled back against the wall as if under the impact of a violent blow. *Was* it coincidence, or something much more sinister? Because who was there, apart from Evan, who knew where she was and that this was the first time she had been left alone? Who—apart from Evan?

'Oh, God!'

It had crossed her mind before, but only vaguely, and she had dismissed it as nonsense. Now it seemed as if a searching spotlight had been directed onto things that she had never looked at clearly before.

Evan had invited himself to her father's house; there he had heard Lloyd say that he was going to Japan, and he had apparently intercepted Joe's call. But—her breath caught in her throat—she had only *Evan's* word that it had even been her tormentor on the other end of the line.

It could have been Ellie ringing back, a wrong number—anything. But because he had used the word 'Honey' she had been convinced, knowing that only the police—and the stalker himself—knew of his name for her. Another coincidence that Joe had rung so conveniently when Evan was there?

And the stalker himself. The words beat inside her head like an ominous drumroll. That phone call had been the last straw. It had pushed aside all her doubts about

Evan, pressurising her into taking him on as her protector—but what if it had just been pretence?

'The letter!'

At last she could move, running desperately up the stairs and into Evan's room, wrenching open the wardrobe doors and pulling out the jacket he had worn that day at her flat, steeling her senses against the faint, devastating traces of his aftershave that still clung to the fine cloth. Her fingers shaking, she went through the pockets, a gasping cry of horror escaping her as they closed over the slippery layer of polythene.

'Oh, Evan—no!'

It was still there. Evan hadn't sent it to the police as he had promised. And, of course, when they had got back to her father's Evan had gone into the house first. He had been such a long time that she, poor fool, had panicked. But of course he would have needed that time to take her underwear from the washing line, arrange the pegs as he wanted, and then hide the clothes in her room—he had been upstairs when she came in.

'Oh, Evan...'

Catherine's legs gave way beneath her and she sank onto the bed. He had homed in on her like a hunting cat on its prey—he had brought her here where they were alone, isolated her from everyone she knew—

'Cat!'

She hadn't heard the car arrive or the door open, but suddenly Evan's voice called from the hall below, followed by the sound of the telephone receiver being dropped back onto its rest.

'*Cat*! Where the hell are you?'

She could hear him running up the stairs, getting closer by the second, but she couldn't have moved if she'd tried. She would certainly never have had the time to reach her own room, because the next moment, it seemed, Evan was in the doorway, his face set in a convincing expression of concern.

'The phone?' he said harshly. 'What the—? Cat, did he ring here?'

Too numbed by shock to care any more, Catherine lifted her head to stare at him, her eyes shadowed and dull.

'Did he ring?' she echoed blankly. '*He*? Why ask when you know the answer?'

'Then he—' But she couldn't let him continue.

'*He!*' she said again. 'Oh, Evan, isn't it time to drop the act? I know.'

'What act?'

Pain stabbed straight to her heart at the thought that he could appear so convincing when he must realise he had been caught out. Even now he couldn't stop pretending, had to continue the bitter farce.

'What the hell are you talking about, Cat? What do you know?'

Savage tears burned her eyes like acid, but she wouldn't let them fall. Unable to speak, she could only hold out the letter, still wrapped in its protective polythene.

'Oh, that!'

There was actually relief in his eyes. Did he think she hadn't worked it all out?

'No—I didn't hand it over to the police, but I had other, more important things on my mind. I had—'

'Oh, I bet you had!' Pain found her voice for her. 'I know what "important things" you had on your mind! You wanted to get me alone so that you could work on me—seduce me.'

'It wasn't like that!'

Bitter devastation and blind, burning fury swept through Catherine's mind in a devastating mixture, white-hot and fierce as any potent alcohol. The agony of knowing how he had betrayed her trust was the worst wound of all.

How could he keep up this pretence? Even now, he still wore that mask of innocence. The strength of despair got her to her feet and even took her the few steps across the room towards him.

'How was it, then Evan? Tell me—or, rather, no, don't tell me any more of your lies. Don't claim that you're indifferent to me because I won't believe you. Beth told me—'

'Damn her loose little tongue!'

Evan's outburst dried the words in her throat, but she wouldn't have been able to utter them anyway because the final, terrible piece of the whole, ugly jigsaw had just fallen into place.

Last November—Beth had said that Evan had first seen her on television last November. Joe's first letter had arrived in December.

'Aren't you going to deny what your sister said, Evan?' She couldn't believe that that hard, brittle voice was her own.

'What's to deny?' He lifted his shoulders in a shrug of terrible indifference. 'Knowing Beth, she'll have told the truth.'

At least he was prepared to be honest about that, if nothing else. There was a sour taste in Catherine's mouth and she felt sick at heart.

'And what about the rest, Evan? What about kissing me and walking away?'

As he had kept her mesmerised in the past with just the force of his eyes, so now she found she could hold his gaze, seeing how wide and dark his irises had become, with just a thin line of blue-green at the outer edge.

'Can you really do that? Are you truly so unmoved by me?'

'Cat—' Evan's voice was low and rough. 'Don't do this.'

But his use of that double-edged nickname was the final push she needed to take her over the edge of restraint and into a dark pit of boiling hatred and uncontrollable need for revenge—revenge for the cold-blooded manipulation of her heart and feelings, for the fear she had endured all these months, for the aching yearning that had racked her body—but most of all for the bitter anguish of his betrayal of her trust.

Letting the letter fall to her feet unnoticed, she reached out slowly and trailed soft fingertips gently down his cheek, a tiny flicker of triumph flashing through her as she saw him flinch, saw those aquamarine eyes widen in shock. Deliberately she repeated the gesture, making her caress even more tantalisingly gentle, letting it trail down to the open neck of his black polo shirt.

'Are you indifferent to this?' she murmured huskily.

'Yes.' Evan's response came in a voice that was disappointingly, almost insultingly firm.

'I see.'

She nodded slowly, consideringly, letting her tongue slip out to lick her lips in the instinctively sensual gesture of a lazy, sun-warmed cat, and moved closer, almost but not quite touching him.

'And this?'

Her hands moved from his throat to his hair, lingering for a moment, curling in the dark, silky strands, then sliding down, down again. One slipped in under his collar, caressing his throat once more, while the other traced tiny, delicate patterns over his chest, feeling his heartbeat quicken under her touch before she let a single finger run along the thick leather belt that encircled his narrow waist, pausing to let it rest on the metal buckle.

'Does this leave you unmoved?'

Evan swallowed hard.

'Yes...' This time it was lower than before, sounding shaken, much less confident, and Catherine allowed herself a small, triumphant smile before moving in for the kill.

'Well, now—how about—?'

Both arms went round his waist, her heart thudding painfully as she felt his tension, the involuntary clenching of the powerful muscles under her hands. Her body barely touched his, but she could not be unaware of the swollen evidence of the effect she was having on him, the response he couldn't hide, and her smile grew as she rubbed her soft cheek against the side of his face, feeling the roughness of the day's growth of beard abrade her skin.

'What about this?' She whispered against his ear, flicking her tongue softly against its outer edge. 'Does this do nothing for you?'

Evan's only response was a wordless, indecipherable sound deep in his throat.

'What was that? A yes or a no?'

Her lips were so close to his ear now that they brushed warmly against his skin as she spoke, and as she stood on tiptoe to reach her teasing position she had to lean lightly against him in order to keep her balance, the heat of his body reaching her bare midriff through the thin material of his shirt.

'Tell me, Evan,' she insisted, subtly increasing the pressure of her slender frame against the tautly held muscles of his strong body, deliberately sliding her pelvis across his.

'Oh, God!'

It was a groan of surrender, sending a hot rush of excitement through her as his arms came round her, fierce and strong, clamping tight as steel bands, holding her prisoner.

'Oh, God, Cat, you *know* I'm not indifferent to you— never have been—never.'

And then he was covering her face with kisses, wild, fierce kisses that demanded a response, demanded she meet them halfway.

And that was where Catherine's calculations went wildly astray, because, having come this far, she found that she couldn't pull back, was incapable of calling a halt. She herself had set a match to the searing, blazing need that Evan's touch, his kisses, awoke in her, and now it was raging out of control, heating her blood until it ran white-hot in her veins, seeming to melt all her bones in the inferno of desire so that she collapsed against Evan and would have fallen if he hadn't supported her, swinging her off her feet and carrying her to the bed where he lay down beside her, still holding her tight, crushed against his strength.

'You don't know how hard it's been, Cat, to pretend— to act as if I don't feel anything.' Evan's voice was rough, raw and husky with passion, and she could only hear it dimly through the roar of her blood, her heart pounding frantically.

'But I do—I know.'

Oh, God, she *knew*! Hadn't she had to endure the same restraint, force herself to pretend just like him, to conceal the way she felt?

But the time for pretence and concealment was over. She was incapable of hiding anything now. Her uneven breathing, the wild glitter in her eyes, the tiny moans that escaped in response to the touch of his hands or his lips, all communicated the spiralling desire that was threatening to blow her mind apart, the devastating need that had to be assuaged or she felt that she would die.

'Of course you do.' His laugh was low, triumphant, his hands busy with the buttons on her shirt. 'It was there from the start—the tension between us, the spark of something so very special. And now...'

His breath hissed between his teeth as the front of her blouse fell away and his burning eyes took in the soft, creamy flesh, the curves of her breasts above the delicate lace of her bra.

'Oh, God, Cat, but you're so lovely. You've been driving me crazy—I've been out of my mind...'

And if he didn't touch her soon, then *she* would go out of hers! Catherine was unable to hold back the whimper of need that escaped as she writhed beneath the imprisoning weight of his body, a glorious sense of triumph filling her as she heard his choked use of her name.

'*Catherine*—don't! I won't be able— I want this to be as good for you as for me. Let's take it steady—'

'No!'

Steady was not what she wanted. Steady meant waiting, time to think—and she had no room in her mind for second thoughts.

'No, Evan. Love me—love me now!'

The words faded into a sigh as he buried his face in the warm valley between her breasts, his mouth hot on her skin, his hands moving over her body like a skilled musician touching the instrument he loved, drawing from it the glorious sound, the perfect melody that only his expertise could bring. And like some finely tuned violin she responded to his mastery, her sighs and moans blending with his muttered endearments in a concerto of need that was the most emotive composition she had ever heard in her life.

'Cat—I can't believe— I thought I'd never—'

This time his kiss was a sensual assault on her mouth, seeming to draw her soul from her, the possessive invasion of his tongue inflaming her body further with its echo of the deeper, more intimate invasion she yearned for.

'More...' she murmured against his lips, and heard his soft laughter.

'More what, darling?' he questioned thickly. 'More of this?'

Once more his kiss sent her senses reeling.

'Or this?'

The urgent pressure of his hands on her breasts had her gasping his name, straining desperately to get closer to him, her own fingers tugging at his clothes, stripping them from him with his willing assistance, wriggling free of her own until, with a sigh of pure happiness, she was naked against him.

'Or perhaps this is what you want...'

Those tormenting fingers moved lower, seeking the core of her femininity, awakening the deepest need of all, the longing that only his complete possession could subdue.

'Yes,' she sighed, opening to him completely, all her fears and doubts washed away on the burning tide of passion, as the boiling flood of lava pouring from a volcano swept aside everything that came into its path. 'Oh, Evan—yes.'

Only then did he move over her, holding her hard against him, lifting her body for the thrust of his. And in the moment that the two of them became one Catherine's soaring heart gloried in both the sense of yielding to his strength and the knowledge that in the same second that she submitted so completely, *she* also had total power over him.

She was the one who had brought him to such a pitch, to the point where all words deserted him and there was only the primitive, passionate communication of their bodies coming together as one.

It was a long, long time before her breathing slowed and her eyes cleared, but in the end, bit by bit, with a terrible sense of inevitability, her thoughts cleared of the burning haze that had filled them, and cold, cruel reason returned. Slowly and unwillingly, but as surely as the cool evening air crept over her sweat-slicked body, the chill of realisation slid into her mind, bringing home to her the awful truth.

Dear God, what had she done? If she had been flirting with danger before, then this time she had been playing with the devil, and she had actually opened the door wide and invited him in.

She had wanted to prove one way or another that Evan wasn't sexually indifferent to her—well, she'd certainly done that! But she hadn't looked beyond the moment of proof, or thought about what it might mean to her. Because Evan's overwhelming response had shown that far from being indifferent he was, in fact, very, very attracted to her—physically at least—and, by his own admission, the sort of sexual passion that he felt for her was what the stalker would also feel.

Nausea crashed over her in bitter, dangerous waves, and, shivering violently, she leapt out of bed, reaching desperately for the nearest thing at hand to cover her nakedness.

'What is it?'

Disturbed by her movement, Evan lifted his dark head from the pillow, his look of satiated pleasure fading, his eyes narrowing swiftly as he registered her white, shocked face.

'Cat, darling—what's wrong?'

'Wrong?' With a jerky, nervous movement, Catherine pulled the navy blue towelling dressing-gown closed around her waist, belting it tightly. 'Wrong? I'll tell you what's wrong—it's you!'

'Me?'

Oh, God, the robe was a terrible mistake. It was Evan's, of course, and still bore the painfully evocative scent of his body, making her want to close her eyes against the bitterness of the memories that ripped through her. But she had to endure the agony. Anything was better than facing him—facing the terrible truth about him—while made more vulnerable than ever by her nakedness.

'Yes, you, damn you! You're him, aren't you? All this time you've deceived me, lied to me, pretended to protect me, when really *you* were Joe all the time!'

'Joe? Cat—no!'

Oh, why wouldn't he just admit it? Why did he still keep up the pretence, even now? Catherine's heart felt as if it was tearing into tiny pieces, and then, just at the moment when she was least able to bear it, the full extent of her foolishness broke over her like a tidal wave.

It wasn't just the dreadful fact of his betrayal that had almost destroyed her—it was the appalling, devastating sense of loss, of having something beyond price taken from her. And now she knew what that something was. Because the real, the numbing truth was that she loved Evan. She didn't quite know when or how it had happened, but she loved him blindly, totally, with all the strength of which her female heart was capable.

But how could she? How could she love someone so callous, someone so deceitful—so sick? How could she give her heart to someone who had made her life hell for so long?

'Cat—you can't possibly think—'

'Don't speak to me! Don't come near me—or say a word. I don't want to hear it. I hate you—I *hate* you!'

'Cat—listen to me—'

'No!'

As Evan made a move to get out of bed her nerve broke once and for all, and she turned and fled, out of the room and down the stairs, knowing from the sounds behind her that Evan was coming after her, pausing only to pull on his jeans. In the hall she froze, not knowing where to turn, what to do. Evan was close behind her, his longer legs dealing with the steps far more swiftly than hers had done.

He had just reached the hall when the telephone rang, its shrill sound seeming to shatter the tension in the air as a soprano's voice could splinter glass. For a couple of long, taut seconds they simply stared at it, then Evan turned his head, sea-coloured eyes locking with blue, his gaze disturbingly intent.

'Answer it!' she flung at him, her voice harsh with distress. 'Go on—answer it. After all, it can't be Joe now, can it?'

It was the perfect opportunity to escape, but in spite of herself something made her stay, to watch and listen as Evan snatched up the receiver.

'Yes?'

For some seemingly endless moments he listened hard, his eyes going once to Catherine's apprehensive face, and a strange, unreadable expression settling on his strongly carved features as he held the receiver out to her.

'Who is it?' she asked suspiciously, and his mouth curled into a bitter travesty of a smile.

'The seventh cavalry,' he murmured cynically. 'The police. I think you'd better listen to what they have to say.'

His face told her everything without a word needing to be spoken, and she knew before she took the phone from him just what she was going to hear, the knowledge freezing her heart, making her blood run icy cold.

It was just as she had suspected. The police had had a lucky break—two telephone calls by the stalker had been made from the same place, and someone had remembered seeing a man hanging around. She had even been able to give them an excellent description. Fingerprints on the one letter Catherine had handed over had confirmed the identification. They knew exactly who they were looking for. They'd be in touch when there was anything more to report.

'Thanks.'

Her voice was as numb and lifeless as the fingers that let the telephone drop with a disturbing clatter. Drawing a deep breath, she nerved herself to face Evan, meeting the icy blaze of his eyes with a terrible sense of desolation.

'Well?' he demanded harshly. 'So what can you tell me about this Lewis Carrington?'

'Corrigan,' Catherine corrected flatly, miserably aware of the way that his mishearing of the name revealed just how angry he was. 'Lewis Corrigan. You remember that I told you Ellie had married again, and her husband had two sons—Geoff and Lewis. I met them both at the wedding, and Lewis made something of a play for me—he was very persistent, very determined, but I didn't like him at all. There was something—shifty about him, and I—rather made my feelings plain.'

She shivered at the memory. So that was when it had all begun. But Lewis was in the past—in the present she still had Evan to deal with.

'And now tell me how Ellie knew where we were, so that she could let it slip so easily? Telepathy, perhaps?'

'No.' Catherine flinched inside at the lash of bitter sarcasm on Evan's tongue, fear and shame making it impossible to meet his molten eyes. 'I rang her from the services on the journey up here. I didn't know the address, but I told her we were going to somewhere in Lincolnshire. She must have said something by mistake, and Lewis tracked me down.'

It had taken him a week to do so, and then, by some terrible coincidence, he had had to ring at the one moment that Evan wasn't at the farm. As a result of which she'd accused him falsely, had him tried and condemned without real evidence.

'Evan—I'm so sorry.'

A month—a week—even a day ago, if someone had told her that the stalker would be exposed, his identity revealed and his malign influence removed, leaving her free to live her life again, she would have been ecstatic, scarcely able to believe her luck.

Now the thing she had most longed for had come about, and all she could feel was a terrible, aching sense of despair, of bitter loss at the thought of the appalling accusations she had flung at Evan, the dreadful way she had treated him, as a result of which, she was sure, he would no longer want anything more to do with her.

'I'm sorry...' she repeated, and headed for the stairs, her footsteps, like her heart, slow and heavy, her thoughts as dreary as the dullest November day.

'Where the hell do you think you're going?' The savagely voiced question stopped her dead.

'Upstairs—to pack.' It was the only thing she could do. She would go back to London, leave Evan in peace, and try to pick up the shattered remains of her life. Wearily she mounted the first step.

'Oh, no you don't.' Evan's hand shot out, clamping hard around her arm, bringing her to an abrupt halt. 'You're not going anywhere.'

'But...' Her protest faded before the blazing anger in his turquoise eyes. 'Evan—it's over.'

'Nothing's over—not until I say it is. Come on, Cat...' His voice changed suddenly, becoming coldly, mockingly cajoling in a way that made a sensation like the trickle of icy water slide down her spine.

'You've had your fun—parading around the house half-naked, flaunting your beautiful body under my nose at every opportunity, cuddling up to me—and I had to act as if I wasn't in the least interested. But now you know I *was* interested—excessively so—and it hurt like hell to pretend otherwise. There's a name for the way you've behaved, Catherine, and it's not a very polite one.'

'But—' She knew she couldn't deny his accusations, and that dangerous use of her full name warned her that he was in no mood to listen even if she tried.

'But nothing, darling.' His tone turned the endearment into an obscenity. 'You tormented me—led me on—and you enjoyed it. Well, you've had your fun and that's fine, but there's a saying that the bill always comes—and as far as you're concerned I'm handing in my account. It's my turn now, sweet Catherine—my turn to take and yours to start giving.'

CHAPTER TWELVE

'BUT you—you—'

Catherine couldn't get the words out.

'Just now—you—'

Evan laughed. 'Do you think that was enough? That was just a taste—an appetiser. It didn't quench my hunger, only encouraged it—making me keen for more.'

Catherine could only stare at him, seeing with a terrible sense of dread the hard set of his mouth, cold anger drawing it into a thin straight line, the inimical glint in his eyes. The man she loved had been vindicated, proved innocent of the dreadful things she had suspected, so she should have been happy, but happiness was the exact opposite of the emotion she was feeling.

Looking back at her behaviour through Evan's eyes, seeing it as he must see it, she could be in no doubt as to how he must now feel about her, and that knowledge made her want to fold her arms around herself, hold herself together, because deep inside she felt as if she was slowly falling apart.

'You can't force me to stay. I'll leave—'

'You'll leave when I say and not before. Remember, we're miles from the nearest village, and I have the car keys right here.' He patted his jeans pocket to emphasise his point.

'I'll call a taxi.' Defiance was the only way she could find to hide her pain.

'Do that,' he dismissed with a cruel smile. 'And when it gets here I'll tell the driver that it's just a lovers' tiff—that you'd be heartbroken if you went through with it. I'd beg him to help me keep you here until you see sense.'

He meant it too—that or worse. The look in his eyes told her so.

'But you can't keep me here!'

'Can't I?' Suddenly, surprisingly, Evan seemed to lose interest in the tormenting game. 'Oh, for God's sake—go and get dressed!'

Catherine had forgotten that she was still wearing only his navy blue robe, the loose neck gaping widely now, revealing the curves of her breasts, the soft skin still marked with the red brands of his passion.

'But I thought—'

'You thought what? That because I said I wanted you, I meant right this minute?' The taunting gleam in his eyes intensified worryingly. 'Now, there's an idea . . .'

He took a menacing step towards her, but when Catherine shrank back fearfully his expression changed dramatically.

'Oh, for God's sake!' His voice was rough and raw. 'Not now, Cat. Damn you—go and get dressed!'

In the bathroom, Catherine turned on the shower and stood underneath it for a very long time, letting the hot water pound down on her head so fiercely that it was almost impossible to think. It might have seemed as if she was using the heat and the force of the shower to try to erase all traces of Evan's touch from her body, but in her heart she knew that that was impossible. The marks on her body might vanish, but he had invaded her heart and her mind in a way that was totally ineradicable.

Besides, she knew that she didn't really want to remove all trace of him from her life. She loved Evan absolutely, without reservation and without any hope of redemption. She loved him so much that she would accept whatever crumbs he threw her way. If the physical passion he had shown her was all that he offered, then she was weak enough to settle for that.

She lingered upstairs for as long as she dared, but knew that she couldn't avoid Evan for ever. Sooner or later she would have to face him, and so, taking her courage in both hands, she pulled on a simple black linen dress and went down.

She found Evan in the sitting-room where, in spite of the fact that the French windows were wide open, not a trace of a breeze stirred the heavy, humid atmosphere of the evening. Evan was slumped in his chair, a loose white shirt pulled on over the denim jeans, its buttons left unfastened all the way down the front, and he had a half-full tumbler in his hand.

'Want one?' He waved the glass at her as she came in.

'No, thanks—well, all right. Yes, some wine would be nice.'

Perhaps the alcohol would help to ease the terrible edgy feeling, like pins and needles inside her mind.

'It won't work, you know.'

Evan had got to his feet, heading for the drinks cabinet.

'The change of image,' he added at her puzzled frown, nodding towards the calf-length black dress. 'All very modest and decorous, but you forget that I know the truth. I'm very well aware of the real Cat underneath the outer appearance, so the nun's-habit-look doesn't convince me.'

'That wasn't why I chose it.'

'No?'

He looked decidedly sceptical, and Catherine nerved herself for further sardonic taunts, but surprisingly none came. Instead, Evan simply passed her her drink and went silently back to his chair.

'Ellie rang while you were in the shower,' he said abruptly. 'The police had been round to see her.'

That distracted Catherine from the disturbed feelings that had resulted from the brief, electric contact with his hand as she took her glass.

'What did she say? She must be in a terrible state, now she knows it was Lewis.'

'She was. I said you didn't blame her, and that you'd ring her tomorrow and tell her so yourself.'

It was a command, not a suggestion, Catherine realised unhappily. He wanted to keep her in isolation for one more night.

'Would you like something to eat?'

The thought of food made her stomach churn painfully. 'No, thanks—I'm not hungry.'

'Neither am I—for food...'

The slanted, sidelong glance from those sea-coloured eyes made Catherine shift uncomfortably in her seat, but then, unexpectedly, Evan's expression changed abruptly and he looked down into his glass, turning it round and round in his strong fingers.

'I owe you an apology.'

Catherine's head came up sharply. Was he beginning to come round at last?

'Oh, not for that—' he'd read her expression easily and accurately '—anything you got, you asked for a thousand times over. But even so, I should have been more responsible. I was knocked off balance, to say the least, so I didn't stop to think about protection.'

Neither had she, Catherine realised shakily. Crazily, stupidly, it hadn't even crossed her mind. She had been flirting with danger, indeed—she had taken every possible risk imaginable. And the worst threat had been to her heart.

'But I want you to know that I wouldn't willingly put you at risk. I've never been one for messing around indiscriminately. I'm not *that* irresponsible—and next time I'll be more prepared.'

Next time. The words repeated dully inside Catherine's head. He was so sure that there would be a next time—that she wouldn't be able to refuse him.

But, after all, why shouldn't he be? Hadn't she already admitted to herself that she would take whatever he offered, even something with so little feeling behind it? And Evan felt nothing—he couldn't treat her this way if he cared even in the slightest.

Suddenly, from the corner of her mind, came a memory of the first day at Dragon Farm, when, up in her room, she had unpacked her things. Having emptied the case she had brought from her flat, she had turned to the plastic bag Evan had filled at the last minute while she was collecting things from the bathroom in her father's house.

Most of its contents had been supremely practical—her nightdress, slippers, dressing-gown—but right at the bottom had been something soft and furry—the ancient, well-loved teddy bear she had had since she was three. Recalling that moment, Catherine suddenly found herself looking at Evan in a very different way. Could the man who had shown such thoughtfulness then really be as hard as he seemed now?

'Evan,' she said tentatively, 'you once told me that if I asked about your past—about women—' she couldn't bring herself to use the word lovers '—that you'd tell me.'

'Of course, you've a right to know.' His tone made it plain that he believed she was asking because of what he'd said, because she wanted to be sure of her own sexual safety, but to Catherine it was even more important than that. 'Ask away.'

'Was there ever someone special? Someone you thought—'

'Of a future with? Marriage? If all I'd wanted was a pretty face, and a warm body in my bed at night, then I suppose I could have picked any one of the girls I've known. But I always wanted more than that. I've always yearned for the great passion—the sort of love your mother was to your father, or the prince to the Little Mermaid in that fairy story you talked of.'

'The great passion'—every word seemed to stab at her already desolated heart.

'And if you find her—?'

'Not *if* Cat—that's not the problem. The real worry is—'

She never knew what he was going to say, because in that moment the French windows banged loudly and the dark figure of a man appeared, etched against the setting sun. As Catherine stared at his lank fair hair, the cold, dead-looking grey eyes, her heart leapt into her throat.

'Hello, Honey,' he said, and, hearing him, she felt all the blood rush from her cheeks, leaving them ashen and drawn as she pressed a hand to her mouth to hold back a cry of distress.

At her side, Evan was on his feet at once, but he froze at Lewis Corrigan's words.

'I said I'd find you,' the man who called himself Joe went on. 'And here I am.'

'And you can just get straight out again,' Evan put in, his voice coldly dangerous.

Corrigan turned a swift, blazing glare on the other man, before turning his attention back to Catherine.

'You shouldn't have betrayed me, Honey. I told you what would happen if you were unfaithful.'

'I— No!' Panic filled her at the thought of the threats he had made, the terrible things he'd said he would do to any other man she showed an interest in.

'Don't be a fool, Corrigan.' Evan's icily scathing tones clashed with Catherine's cry of fear. 'The police know who you are—'

'You keep out of this,' Lewis snapped, sliding one hand into his jacket pocket. 'This is between my girl and—'

'But that's where you're wrong,' Evan cut in on him. 'Catherine's not your girl—she's mine.'

'What?' It was a vicious snarl, his face that of a hunted animal as he shook his head wildly. 'No—no—she's mine.'

With a swift movement he came forward to catch hold of Catherine's wrist, meaning to drag her to her feet.

'Don't touch her!'

Evan lunged forward just as Catherine saw Lewis's other hand come out of his pocket with the flash of something metallic in its grasp. Her mind reeled at the thought of those terrible threats being carried out, the violence he had threatened being turned on—

'Evan, *no*! He's got a knife!'

She didn't know if he had heard her, only that Corrigan had let her go and swung round, turning his attention to defending himself as Evan launched himself on him.

'No one will have you but me, Honey! I'll kill anyone who tries to take you.'

She had no doubt that he meant it. He was totally obsessed—crazy.

'Evan—don't!'

Evan's muttered response to her cry of fear was almost inaudible, but she caught the word ''mermaid'', and a fresh wave of horror broke over her as she was suddenly back in her flat on the day he had taken her there. As if it was a scene from a film, replaying on the screen of her mind, she could see his intent, deeply serious expression, hear his voice saying, 'If I loved someone, I wouldn't think twice. If she was the one . . . I'd give my life for her.'

'Oh, God! Evan be careful—please—I love you!'

Fear blurred her vision, so that all she could make out was a tangle of movement, of flailing limbs and wild punches, but then the knife went flying and landed with a clatter on the paving stones of the patio. As her fearful gaze followed its path, blinking hard to refocus her eyes, she saw the dark uniformed figure who bent to pick it up, pocketing it carefully before he and two others like him came to Evan's aid.

With the combined force of all four of them against him Corrigan didn't stand a chance, and a few minutes later it was over, with the man who had called himself Joe held firmly in the secure grip of two powerful policemen while the other, the officer she had first seen, was helping Evan to his feet.

'Evan...' Catherine's voice was weak and uneven, but he caught it and turned his head in her direction.

'I'm fine, Cat,' he said quietly, but with no trace of a smile on his face. His breathing was ragged, his hair all over the place, his shirt had been torn and there was an ugly mark on one strong cheekbone that would be a colourful bruise in a while, but otherwise he was unhurt. 'I'm fine,' he repeated.

'Thank God.'

Not knowing whether the feeling of faintness that swept over her was delayed shock or overwhelming relief, Catherine sank back into her chair and closed her eyes, giving in to the momentary weakness. She was only dimly aware of the brief conversation between Evan and the police, her bruised mind unable to take in any of the details, but at last she heard the sound of their departure; they were taking Corrigan with them. The door closed, and then she and Evan were alone once more.

'It's all right, Cat.' Evan's voice was softly soothing. 'It's all over—for good this time. Corrigan's gone, and he'll not be back. The police followed him here, so they saw and heard everything—enough to charge him with anyway. So you're quite safe. You can open your eyes.'

But Catherine didn't know if she dared. It wasn't the thought of seeing Lewis that troubled her any more, but the fear of what she might see in Evan's face, in his eyes—or, rather, what she might *not* see.

Had she really heard him make the reference to the Little Mermaid? And if she had, had he meant it in the way that, in the heat of the moment, she had taken it, giving it a significance that was so intensely personal?

'Cat—look at me.'

Slowly, fearfully, she opened her eyes, but couldn't meet his searching gaze as he knelt beside her chair.

'Th—thank you for coming to my rescue like that,' she managed to whisper. 'It was very brave.'

Out of the corner of her eye she saw his dismissive shrug.

'It was what I'm paid to do.'

'Then in that case I'm not paying you enough.'

Suddenly realising what he had said, her head came up swiftly, meeting those aquamarine eyes head-on for the first time, seeing their impenetrable darkness.

'But I'm not paying you at all! You said you'd volunteered!'

'Ah!'

For the first time Evan actually looked at a loss, and that was so unexpected, so unlike his usual cool self-confidence, that Catherine allowed the tiniest glimmer of hope to filter into the bleakness of her thoughts.

'So I did.'

'Why?' Catherine sat forward in her chair, determined to press home her advantage.

'Why did I volunteer?' He was playing for time, she realised, and the gleam of hope grew brighter.

'Did Beth tell me the truth, Evan? Did you see me on the show—on television? Did you know who I was that first time you came to my father's house?'

'Yes...' It was so soft, muffled by the way he had looked down at the floor, that she almost missed it and couldn't be absolutely certain that he'd said what she thought.

'What did you say?'

'I said yes!'

Evan's head came up in a rush, and Catherine reeled back, stunned by the force of feeling blazing in those sea-coloured eyes.

'Yes, I knew who you were—at least, I knew that your father's daughter was the Catherine Davies I'd seen on the TV screen. And, yes, Beth was telling the truth when she let that particular feline out of the bag. I'd been knocked for six simply by the sight of you, and my kid sister knew that. She teased me mercilessly about it, even threatened to write to you at the studios in my name, and made sure I couldn't forget *your* name—not that I could have done if I'd tried.

The look he turned on her was so boyishly wry and appealing that Catherine's heart seemed to turn over inside her in response.

'The security job for your father was an unexpected bonus. I'd originally planned to negotiate the contracts and leave all the practical work to the men I employ, but when I realised just who he was—and there was no doubt about that; he's so proud of you that he talked about you non-stop from our very first meeting—I suddenly became very involved in the installation work in the hope of somehow getting to meet you.'

That grin surfaced once more, wider this time—heartstoppingly so.

'My crew thought I'd gone completely off my head—usually I leave them to it, but suddenly I was there every day. But it worked in the end. That night your dad said he had to leave early, I practically bit his hand off with the speed with which I suggested I went home with him—I was desperate to see what you were like in the flesh.'

'You certainly didn't give that impression,' Catherine couldn't help interjecting.

'I know—but that's because I was so completely thrown by what I found. I never thought I'd meet *you* right away. When Lloyd said he was concerned about his daughter, I thought he meant a younger child—from a second marriage, perhaps. Instead, I'd barely walked through the door when there you were—more beautiful than I'd ever imagined, but about as approachable as an iceberg.'

'I was scared.' Secretly, Catherine hugged that "beautiful" to her, letting it warm her bruised heart.

'I know. It was pretty obvious that something was wrong, but I didn't know what, and when I found out what was happening I knew I couldn't let you know the real reason I was there—you'd had more than enough of crazed fans harassing you.'

'But you weren't crazed!'

'I certainly wasn't the sanest I've ever been in my life.' Evan laughed. 'I just wanted to get to know you, and I desperately wanted to touch you—kiss you—but I thought that if I tried you'd run a mile—a thousand miles.'

'So that's why—'

'Why I started to make love to you and then stopped? Partly—it wasn't quite as calculated as that. When you fell into my arms I lost my head. I kissed you because I just couldn't help myself—but then you responded so innocently, and I knew I just couldn't take advantage. You were so vulnerable, so trusting—*too* trusting. *I* knew that you could trust me—but you had to learn that for yourself.'

This time Evan's smile was very gentle, its warmth acting like a soothing balm on the wounds she had felt.

'You were running scared, Cat. Perhaps I went rather too far in warning you off, but I was afraid that you would have trusted anyone who offered you help.'

'I'm not that naïve!' Catherine protested. 'I sensed something different about you from the start, believe me...'

Her attempt at laughter was shaky, because she knew just what she had sensed at that first meeting. Even then she had known, on some deep-down, intuitive level, that

Evan was the man with whom she would ultimately fall in love—though she hadn't recognised that feeling for what it was.

'I don't usually fall into just anyone's arms like that.'

An irrepressibly triumphant light gleamed in Evan's eyes, making them glow warmly.

'I hoped it was something like that, but I couldn't be sure, and it would have been so very wrong of me to take advantage—especially when we came here and it seemed that you suspected I might actually be the stalker. Then it became even more important that I kept my distance.'

'So you pretended that you were indifferent?'

'Yeah—' Evan's mouth twisted slightly '—you'll never know how hard it was to keep up that particular front. I've had so many cold showers this past week, it's a wonder I'm not deep-frozen.'

'Oh, but I do know—I understand perfectly.'

He hadn't said he loved her, or anything like it, but this was more than she had allowed herself to hope for.

'I felt that way too—I do now.'

She desperately wanted to touch him, would have done so, but the frown he turned on her made her draw back.

'Do you remember when you told me that you were afraid of being like your mother—of inheriting her inability to build a lasting relationship?'

'Yes . . .'

The answer came warily. She didn't know what this had to do with anything.

'Well, I want you to know that I don't think you need to worry. You may have Melissa's dramatic flair—both in your career and your decorating tastes—but in terms of emotions you're much more like your father. You're loyal—to Lloyd, to Will; you wouldn't let me think any ill of him at all. And you even fought for Ellie like a tigress, so there's no doubt in my mind that when you fall in love, it'll be as your father did—for life. Which brings me to my point. If I ask you a question, will you answer with complete honesty?'

The sudden deep seriousness of his tone, the intensity of that turquoise gaze, the way a muscle had tightened in his jaw, all gave her warning that he had been leading up to this point since the conversation began.

'Of course.' Because she had some suspicion of what he meant, her voice was uneven but still rang with conviction.

'When Corrigan was here—when you saw the knife—did you mean what you said?'

There could be only one thing she had said that was so very important to him to know about.

'That I loved you? Yes, I meant it.' What point was there in denying it now? It must be stamped on every feature, burning in her eyes.

Evan closed his eyes briefly, his sigh one of deep relief.

'Thank God!' he breathed. 'I thought you only wanted me for my body.'

'Oh, Evan!' It was a cry of distress. 'I never meant—I'm so sorry— I—'

She broke off abruptly as she saw that his eyes were open again, and they were filled with such tender laughter that she felt her heart leap in response.

'I know, sweetheart— I *know*! I think I always did—even when you did your seductive siren act and then dropped me cold. I should have realised what was going through your mind—how confused you felt—but I was angry. I felt used—and I was hurt that you should even suspect that I was that—'

'No.' Catherine laid her fingers across his mouth to silence him. 'No, Evan—that's behind us. He's gone, and, please God, he won't come back.'

'He'll regret it if he does,' Evan growled against her restraining fingers. 'He'll have me to contend with.'

'For how long?' She had told herself that she wouldn't ask the question, but now she couldn't hold it back.

'How long?' Evan blinked hard in confusion, then he pulled away from her hand, looking deep into her eyes. 'For the rest of your life if you'll have me. I promised I'd never leave you alone again, and I meant it.'

'You—'

Catherine could only stare at him, her expression a mixture of delight and disbelief, and, seeing it, Evan groaned, shaking his head in self-reproach.

'I haven't said it, have I? All this time I've been explaining why I behaved as I did, and I never said the words.'

'What words?'

Catherine's teasing was light, because now she knew exactly what he meant. She also knew that really there was no need for him to say anything. Deep down, she'd known what he felt for her in the moment that he had flung himself at Lewis—heedless of the knife, of the danger to himself—for her sake. 'If I loved someone, I wouldn't think twice'. And he'd just proved that those words were so much more than mere bravado.

Actions spoke louder than words, but all the same she wanted to hear him say it. 'Tell me,' she encouraged softly.

'The most important words I've ever spoken in my life.' Evan's voice was husky with emotion. 'I love you, Cat—I love you with all my heart. I think I fell head over heels the moment that I saw you on the TV screen, but if I had any doubts then they vanished when I arrived at your father's house. There you were in an old, faded shirt and torn jeans, not a scrap of make-up, and no woman had ever looked lovelier in my eyes. I knew then that, like your father, I could only ever live my life with one love—and that love had to be you.'

'So even if I hadn't asked you to help...' She was so shaken by the power of his declaration that she could hardly get the words out.

'I'd have stayed,' Evan declared emphatically. 'I could never have left that house without knowing that I would see you again. If you hadn't asked me then I'd have set up camp in the garden—on your doorstep—anywhere. I couldn't leave you then, and I never will again. As I said, you didn't conscript me—I volunteered.'

He had moved closer with every word he spoke, so that now all she had to do was tilt her head and her lips brushed his. Immediately it was as if an electric charge had surged between them as Evan gathered her up into his arms, crushing her mouth under his, communicating through the force of his kiss the strength of the love that he had expressed in words just moments before.

Catherine surrendered willingly, knowing at last that Evan had been right. In matters of the heart she was her father's daughter. Evan was the one, the only man for her, and would be for the rest of her life.

At long last Evan released her, but only to come and sit on the arm of the chair beside her, still holding her close. Catherine sighed contentedly and smiled her joy straight into his eyes.

'I'm so glad you "volunteered", because that means you can't object if you think I'm making excessive demands on you,' she murmured softly, letting the way her body was pressed up against his make her meaning only too plain.

Evan's response was immediate, the passionate desire that blazed in his eyes warming her right to the bottom of her heart and making her blood flow more swiftly through her veins.

'I certainly can't.' He smiled back. 'But I seem to recall you admitting that you weren't paying me enough.'

'I'm not paying you anything!'

'Not money, perhaps—but I'm perfectly willing to take my rewards in kind.'

'What sort of reward were you thinking of?'

She knew only too well what he meant. The touch of his hands was warm and possessive, swiftly changing to urgent demand as they moved over her body.

Leaning forward, Evan put his mouth very close to her ear.

'Why don't we go upstairs?' he whispered softly. 'And then I can show you exactly what I have in mind.'

Coming Next Month

HARLEQUIN PRESENTS®

#1821 UNWANTED WEDDING Penny Jordan
(Top Author)
Rosy had to be married within three months. Guard Jamieson was successful, sexy—and single. With no other candidate available to walk her down the aisle, it looked as if Rosy would have to accept Guard's offer to help her out.

#1822 DEADLY RIVALS Charlotte Lamb
(Book Two: SINS)
When Olivia first met Max she was utterly captivated. But Max was her father's business enemy and she was forbidden to see him again. Four years later she agreed to marry Christos, Max's nephew. Then Max returned to claim her....

#1823 TWO'S COMPANY Carole Mortimer
(9 TO 5)
Juliet's boss has left her half his company but she has to share it with Liam, his son, who is sure that she seduced his father. Nor does she want him to know that she was engaged to his despised younger brother. Will he find out her dark secret?

#1824 A SAVAGE BETRAYAL Lynne Graham
(This Time, Forever)
Mina and Cesare had met again, four years after he rejected her as a gold-digging tramp! Now he was determined to marry her, but only to pursue his revenge on Mina.

#1825 SPRING BRIDE Sandra Marton
(Landon's Legacy: Book 4)
Kyra's father's legacy would allow her to assert her independence. Antonio would help her—but at a price! He wanted to own her completely—and if she succumbed Kyra knew she would never be free again.

#1826 PERFECT CHANCE Amanda Carpenter
(Independence Day)
Mary's life was reasonably happy—until the day Chance Armstrong walked into it! He was offering her the perfect chance for a lot of excitement and the most exciting challenge of all.... He asked Mary to marry him!

To: The Reader

From: The Editor at Harlequin Presents

Subject: #1823 Two's Company
by Carole Mortimer

*Will he find out the secret
she's hidden for so long?*

P.S. Available in July wherever
Harlequin books are sold.

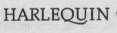

HARLEQUIN PRESENTS®

Mina and Cesare Falcone had met again, four
years after he had rejected her as a gold digger

BUT

He's back!

This time it'll be different

This time it'll be forever!

**#1824 A Savage Betrayal
by Lynne Graham**

Available in July wherever

books are sold

Love can conquer the deadliest for

Indulge in Charlotte Lamb's seven-part series

#1822 DEADLY RIVALS
by Charlotte Lamb

Olivia realized that, to Max Agathios, she was merely the
trophy he had won from his deadly rival. Max wanted to
make war, not love!

Available in July wherever Harlequin books are sold.